A World Quite Round

Also by Gordon Weaver

A World Quite Round

Two Stories and a Novella by
GORDON WEAVER

Louisiana State University Press
Baton Rouge and London   1986

Designer: Christopher Wilcox
Typeface: Times Roman
Typesetter: G & S Typesetters, Inc.
Printer: Thomson-Shore, Inc.
Binder: John Dekker & Sons, Inc.

Publication of this book has been supported by a grant from the National Endowment for the Arts in Washington, D.C., a federal agency.

"Ah Art! Oh Life!" first appeared in *Bennington Review*, No. 8 (September, 1980); "The Parts of Speech" first appeared in *Kenyon Review*, VI (Summer, 1984); and "The Interpreter" first appeared in *Tri-Quarterly*, a publication of Northwestern University (Fall, 1985).

Library of Congress Cataloging-in-Publication Data

Weaver, Gordon.
   A world quite round.

   I. Title.
PS3573.E17W6   1986   813'.54   85-23680
ISBN 0-8071-1291-7
ISBN 0-8071-1326-3 (pbk.)

For Judy, Kristina, Anna, and Jessica.
And for Merle and Jack Michel
And for Janet and Hubie

I cannot bring a world quite round,
Although I patch it as I can.
                    —Wallace Stevens

Contents

A World Quite Round

Ah Art! Oh Life!

Oskar watched Professor Berntsson paint. The Professor's wife watched Oskar. Oskar tried not to show he knew she watched him. The Professor looked only at his canvas on the easel, and at his image in the large mirror propped against the wall; he glanced quickly at the reflection of himself, perched on the high stool, painting, back at the canvas, a portrait of himself painting a self-portrait. Oskar, seated on the sofa, tried to draw the Professor in the big sketchbook. The Professor's wife sat in the overstuffed chair in the far corner of the room, wrapped in an afghan.

Oskar could see everything: the walls hung with paintings, the Professor on his stool, the image of him in the mirror, the incomplete image in oils on the canvas, Mrs. Berntsson bound in her afghan in the overstuffed chair. He waited and tried to draw, confused by trying to look at so many things at once, knowing Mrs. Berntsson would speak whenever the Professor did.

"How are we coming at it?" the Professor said.

"Me or you?" Oskar said. The Professor laughed, put down his brush and rod and palette, wiped his hands on a color-spotted rag. "Yours is neat," Oskar said. "Mine stinks." The Professor laughed again, took the sketchbook from him. "I can't do it like it should look," Oskar said.

"Are you drawing what you see or what you think it should look like?" Oskar knew what Mrs. Berntsson would say when she spoke.

"He's such a lovely boy," she said. "He is such a sweet little boy. He is the prettiest boy."

"Yes, Karin, he is a fine boy," the Professor said. Oskar concentrated on the sketchbook, the thick soft-lead pencil in his fingers. Professor Berntsson said, "The light's going, we'll call it quits maybe, eat some lunch."

"Why can't we just turn on the lights when it gets afternoon?" He knew what Mrs. Berntsson would say when the Professor fell asleep after lunch.

"Oh no, that's not the same light at all." He waved his hand at the light flooding the room from the big windows, explained again how by the time lunch was over the sun would have moved enough to change the light, reduce it to an indirect glow that was not good enough to work in. "Look here," he said to Oskar, "here's something to learn. What you see is not all lines you have to draw. There's color, heh?" He pointed to his incomplete self-portrait on the canvas. "And *tone*. Light and dark when you're drawing in pencil. What do you think the lines you want to draw always are made of? You see?"

"I guess," Oskar said, and tried to see, but could not.

He talked about light when he showed Oskar his paintings. "Do you like to look at pictures?" Oskar said he guessed he did. "Maybe you could be a critic here, huh?"

"Papa's testing you," Hank Berntsson said.

"Hjalmar," his father said, "you go on out and find yourself an honest job, me and this boy are talking about art."

"Papa thinks everyone's an artist," Hank Berntsson said. There was a catch in his speech, as if he were going to stutter, but did not quite.

"Behave yourself, love," his Aunt Kristina said, and kissed Oskar goodbye. She kissed Hank Berntsson and said, "Luck, darling."

"We're already late, Kris," Elsa Berntsson said, and Gene Berntsson said he enjoyed these sentimental partings as much as anyone, but they were going to be late.

"Go, go," their father said. "Here we're interested in more important things." Hank and Elsa and Gene Berntsson kissed their mother goodbye, and they all left with Oskar's Aunt Kristina. Mrs. Berntsson smiled at them, but said nothing.

"What are you looking at when you look?" the Professor said to him. "Do you see just pictures of people and trees and grass?"

"I guess," Oskar said. "I mean it's a picture of a lady. I see it," he said, looking harder to see if there was something more hidden in the picture's colors and tones, a face, figure, shape.

"No," Professor Berntsson said. "Look at the *light*. Always. What I do best, what I do here, is catching the light the special way it is, always. Everything we see is in the light, huh? That's how we see it. See?"

The apartment's walls were covered with his paintings, all but the kitchen and the bathroom. And he had more, unframed canvases stacked on edge in the back of each closet, laid flat on high storage shelves. The Professor blew dust from them, held them up for Oskar to see, made him stand back for correct perspective.

"Did you paint all these? Is it every single picture you ever made?"

The Professor laughed.

"Hundreds more I gave away, and people have bought many. Many. My work is in museums, and schools, here, back in the old country. So many I couldn't count if I tried."

"Neat," Oskar said. "My aunt said you were real famous. She said you were in the Swedish Academy and you were a professor a real long time."

"Kris is very nice," he said, and "I studied at the Swedish Academy. You know what that is? I am not a member. I retired from the Art Institute here probably before you were born. Us Swedes," he said, "we got to stick together, huh?" and laughed.

There were many pictures of Swedish peasants in full costume, gathered for festivals, dancing in circles outdoors, wearing garlands of wildflowers, dancing indoors before huge fireplaces. "Look," he said, "how here it's dusk. Night is coming. See the sky, the air, all filled with the darkness coming? They dance to celebrate a harvest, the end of summer. Here, the light from the fire, see it jumps up there in the rafters to make shadow. See the woman's face red from the fire? It's winter, so they have a party inside with a warm fire."

There were many paintings of small ponds and pools, reedy banks of rivers and lakes, always in the early morning, mists and fogs over the still water. Young women, nude, bathed in the chilly mornings. "Is it just a naked girl there? What, because you can see her hair? I'm sorry, but you don't look correctly."

"No," Oskar said. "I mean I wasn't just looking because she hasn't got her clothes on."

"The special light I get there. Can't you feel how cold the water is? That's the way light comes just after the dawn. Even Zorn didn't do it better."

There were portraits, very old peasant men and women, only their faces, very close-up. They wore caps and bonnets, kerchiefs knotted under their chins, deeply lined faces, lips drawn back over toothless gums. Oskar could not tell if they smiled or were in pain. "Compare the two now. See the sun hitting her right in the face? Of course it's the sun, where else is all that light from? She squints. Here, what time of day is it?"

"Later?" Oskar said.

"Sure. The light is very different. I didn't paint these to make photographs of people."

"Are they real people?"

"Sure. You're right, there's character in a portrait, you can see the whole of the old country here, you're right. That's us there, you and me, your Aunt Kris, where the Swedes all come from, huh? But the technical problem is light, always."

"What's *technical* mean?"

"Means everything," Professor Berntsson said.

They ate lunch from a low coffee table pulled close to Mrs. Berntsson's chair. Oskar knelt on the carpet to eat his sandwich, drink a glass of milk, pretending not to stare at the Professor feeding his wife, poking cereal into her mouth, catching dribbles on her lip with the spoon, wiping her chin with a damp towel. "Open wide, Karin. Ah. Isn't that good? Good for you. You got to eat nice. What a good girl!" Mrs. Berntsson opened her mouth, closed, swallowed, flicking her eyes from her husband to Oskar to the spoon lifting toward her mouth.

Oskar carried the dishes to the kitchen, moved the coffee table back to the sofa while the Professor carried his wife to the bathroom. He sat at one end of the sofa, waited. He listened to the sounds from the bathroom, the Professor's voice, running tap, toilet flushing. He waited, looked at the paintings on the walls, at the glistening paint drying to a glaze on the canvas on the easel, at his own reflection, sitting, waiting, in the mirror propped beyond the easel. "Now, Karin," the Professor said as he lowered her carefully into her chair, tucked the afghan about her, "we'll relax a little," and, to Oskar, "Let's see how we did today."

He prepared himself to talk, keep him awake as long as possible. Beside him on the sofa, Professor Berntsson slumped, hands open and still in his lap, head tilted a bit forward. He blinked frequently, heavy-lidded. So close to him, Oskar saw how very old he was.

The backs of his hands were mottled with liver spots, crosshatched with raised, purple veins. A long tuft of stiff white hair sprouted in the depth of his ear. His mouth sagged beneath his snowy moustache. A last beam of direct light from the windows bounced off the slickness of the Professor's bald crown. His body looked smaller and rounder, softer, arms and legs spindly, thin ankles exposed below his trouser cuffs. Oskar did not look at Mrs. Berntsson, but said something, anything, quickly.

"Pretty neat, I think."

"What's?" the Professor started, looked up sharply.

"What you painted today."

"Ah. Maybe." He leaned forward, raised his rimless spectacles to look at the drying canvas. "Too soon to say," he said, and, "Sometime I'll show you how many studies I drew for this. Sketches."

Oskar looked at the unfinished self-portrait, then at the Professor beside him. They were identical and very different. "I really think it's nifty so far."

"You don't see the problems." The Professor sat back, sighed. His head canted to one side. His breathing was suddenly shallower and faster, a wheezing.

"How old are you?" Oskar said quickly.

"What? Such a question."

"I'm ten. My brother Lars is thirteen already. I can't tell how old old people are. You're older than my Aunt Kristina and my mom and my dad I know. My Aunt Anna's older than my mom, and my mom's older than my Aunt Kristina, and my dad's the same age almost as my mom, but I forget exactly how old. My Uncle Knute was older than Aunt Anna but he got killed in a war a long time ago."

"I don't believe Kris mentioned your uncle," he said.

"My Aunt Anna's the oldest one of my aunts. Lars said he didn't care which one we went to, so I picked my Aunt Kristina."

"You don't say."

"I think she's real pretty."

The Professor laughed a tired laugh. "Do you hear that, Karin?" he said to his wife. Oskar looked at her, saw she watched them.

"How old?" Oskar said. "Really."

"You don't give up. How can I keep my vanity? Can you keep a secret?" Oskar nodded. "Eighty-two." He smiled at Oskar. "See, visit me, you learn something every time."

Oskar forgot to think of something more to say. There was the number eighty-two, but it did not mean anything he could understand. He knew he was ten, his brother Lars thirteen. After that he did not know any ages, his mother and father, his aunts, Hank and Elsa and Gene Berntsson, his dead Uncle Knute who was the oldest somehow, but there were no numbers between himself and his brother and the Professor.

The Professor began to snore. Oskar thought to wake him, ask him quickly and loudly how old his children were, the ages for all the people, but when he turned to him Professor Berntsson was deeply asleep, and Mrs. Berntsson was staring at him, and now she would begin to speak to him alone.

At her vanity, his Aunt Kristina hurried with her makeup; she said they would be miles late. "How's come Mrs. Berntsson's so funny?" Oskar said.

"Funny funny or funny strange?" she said, and, "I think she's the cutest little thing. She's like a little Dresden doll."

Oskar said, "Sometimes she doesn't say anything for a long time, and then she says how nice I am and everything, and then she talked real different when the Professor took a nap after lunch."

"Really?" She leaned close to the vanity's mirror to curl her lashes and apply eyeliner, tweeze a hair from one brow, draw in a thin arc. Her bracelets clattered when she moved her hands. Her rings winked in the sunlight from the bedroom windows. Her dangling earrings jumped as she stroked her long hair.

"I don't like it so much being with all old people all the time," he said.

"Come on," she said, smiled at him in the vanity mirror. "Is your Auntie Krissie old? Hank and Gene and Elsa aren't old, are they? Am I old?" She smiled hard at him in the mirror.

"I think you're pretty."

"Flattery will get you most anything in life, Os," his Aunt Kristina said. The scent of her perfume came into the air when she took the stopper from the vial, dabbed it at her ears, throat, the insides of her wrists, and the heavy sweetness mingling with the smoke from her cigarette burning in an ashtray among the clutter of bottles, brushes, combs, powder boxes. She squinted against the smoke as she took a last puff, a last sip from the coffee cup beside the ashtray.

"I wish I could just stay here all day until you come home from work."

"You can't, Os. Be a sweetheart. Go comb your hair again, I want you to look swell for the Berntssons."

To stay, he said, "Do you think my mom and dad will call today and I can go home tomorrow instead of with the Berntssons?"

"There's always a chance for anything," his Aunt Kristina said. A photograph of his aunt sat on the vanity; he could tell it was her, but it did not look a lot like her. She had photographs and snapshots everywhere in her bedroom, on the walls, the dresser, the bedside tables. They were all of herself.

"You sure were pretty," he said. She looked away from the mirror, lipstick in one hand, Kleenex to blot her lips in the other. He pointed at the portrait on the vanity. "Oh. Well, thank you kindly, sir," she said, and, "That was a million years ago," and closed her lips on the tissue. She was posed before a flowing swath of drapery, lighted from below and behind her, so that the fabric looked like swirling smoke, and cast an intense halo about the hair piled carelessly on top of her head. The frills of the boa that lay below her bare shoulders seemed electrified by the light, to waver and dance. She held the boa in place loosely at her bosom with the fingers of one hand. Her painted nails and swollen lips gleamed blackly in contrast to the soft, dull whiteness of her skin. Her large eyes were wide, moist, not seeming to look at the camera, at anything. "I had that taken to oblige a gentleman friend," she said.

"Was he the gangster?" Oskar said. When she turned fully away from the mirror to look at him, he said, "My dad said once you almost got married with a gangster. Lars believed him, but I didn't," he said because his aunt was not smiling at all.

"He wasn't a *gangster*," she said. "Your old man spouts off when he doesn't know beans, which is only part of the headache he's caused your mama. Serves her right for marrying another squarehead Swede."

"Wasn't he really a gangster?"

"You're too young to understand," his Aunt Kristina said, and, "He happened to know some people who were is all. He introduced me once to Capone. He was a businessman. Your old man should be told to keep his trap shut."

"My dad said he got shot."

"Let's change the subject, Oskar."

"Didn't he get shot by gangsters?"

"My Christ," she said, and now she laughed and smiled hard at him. "Do you pull this twenty questions on everyone or just Aunt Krissie? I'm sorry, Os. Next time you see him, ask your old man if getting shot by a gangster makes you one. That should hold his water."

"Were you married with him?"

She stood up, looked at herself carefully in the mirror, smoothed her dress. "The subject was discussed," she said, "but even the best laid plans can blow up on you."

"Hank Berntsson got shot in the war."

"He got shot *at*. That's why he's so nervous, I told you."

"My Uncle Knute got killed in the war," Oskar said.

She looked at him for a moment before she spoke. "You've got your wars mixed up, Os," she said. "Hank was in this one. My Christ," and she laughed, "I was still wearing bloomers when Knute went off. *Tempus* do *fugit*," she said.

"You're getting married with Hank Berntsson," Oskar said. She turned from the mirror to him, smiling, took his face in her hands, bent toward him.

"Every maiden's hope and prayer," his Aunt Kristina said.

"I wish I could just stay here," Oskar said. He began to cry without wanting to.

"Oh, Ossie," his aunt said, "please, sweet doll-boy, don't blubber. Auntie Krissie can't stand to see you turn on the water-works, please!" She put her head next to his, hugged him.

"My mom said when two people can't get along any more they have to have a divorce. We had to go away to Aunt Anna and you. I wish I could be with my mom and dad and Lars." He began to cry so hard he could not talk. She hugged him tightly, rocked him in her arms.

"Please," she said, "won't you help your auntie? See, I *need* you to help me. I need you to make a real swell impression for me. Won't you be a love and make the Professor and Gene and Elsa just fall in love with you? Please help Krissie, Oskar."

When he could stop crying, he said, "I'll try I guess." She laughed and hugged him again, very tight. "So you can get married with Hank Berntsson and live happy ever after?"

"You could be a quiz kid," she said, and wiped his eyes

and nose and mouth with a Kleenex. "And mum's the word about *gangsters*, okay? Half the trick in life is knowing when to clam up, trust me," his Aunt Kristina said.

"Mum's the word," he said. She hugged and kissed him, then had to wipe off the lipstick on his cheek.

The Professor snored long low snores, stirring the fringe of his snowy moustache with each breath. A blue vein pulsed in the glossed, papery skin at his temple, fluttering movement visible beneath his eyelids. Oskar watched him to avoid looking at his wife in the chair across the room. He had to look at her when she began to speak to him.

"Bad boy," Mrs. Berntsson said. Her voice was very high and clear, like a little girl's. "Dirty boy," she said, "Dirty pig!" There was something like a smile on her tiny face. He could see the perfectly even edges of sparkling white dentures. Her small recessed eyes flashed, her head and torso quivered as she spoke, louder. "You are a dirty, nasty boy!"

"I'm not doing anything," Oskar said. His own voice sounded weak to him, as if he were trying to keep from crying. He knew he could not let himself start to cry. "I'm just sitting here," he said. Professor Berntsson's snoring was very loud when they did not speak.

"Go away. Get out of here right now. Go, dirty thing!" She began to rock in the cocoon of her afghan, as if she meant to get out of the chair, come across the room at him. "*Go!*" she screeched.

"I can't! I have to stay here. I have to visit my aunt to see if my mom and dad have to have a divorce."

"Nasty," she said.

"My Aunt Kristina said I have to stay here all day while she goes to work with Elsa." He tried to talk loud enough to wake the Professor, but his voice was too weak.

"Dirty, dirty," Mrs. Berntsson said with the edges of her false teeth showing.

He stopped answering her. He tried to make himself think

of other people, his mother and father and brother Lars, his Aunt Kristina and his Aunt Anna, of Elsa and Gene and Hank Berntsson, the Professor sleeping beside him, of the dead man killed by gangsters who was not really a gangster his aunt almost married a million years ago, of his Uncle Knute who was killed in the war he mixed up with the one that just was. He tried to think their names and faces, things they had said to him, where each one was this minute, but still he heard Mrs. Berntsson speaking to him.

"Nasty, dirty," she said. He made himself look away. He looked at the propped mirror reflecting himself, hands clutched in his lap, the sleeping Professor, the easel and the Professor's unfinished self-portrait in oils.

In the darkened room, Oskar could see only the darker shape of his aunt bending over him. He heard the tinkle of ice in her highball glass, saw the sudden glow of her cigarette when she drew on it, heard the whooshing sound as she exhaled smoke. "Don't let the bugs bite," she said.

"You have to hear my prayers," he said.

"Lordy. I just bet your mama doesn't miss a night, does she." The end of her cigarette glowed again, and he heard her drink, the ice rattle in the bottom of the glass, her sighing exhale of smoke. She knelt beside the folding cot. Very close, he smelled her perfume, the stale odor of her cigarettes, the tinge of alcohol on her breath from the highball nightcap she had just finished.

"You can say it with me if you remember it," Oskar said.

"I never trust to memory," she said, and he said the Lord's Prayer in Swedish. She said amen with him, but in the dark he could not see if she had folded her hands as he prayed. She laughed. "Who but your mama would teach you that," she said, laughed again.

"What's funny?"

"Nothing. The fact I recall Annie trying to teach me that

hoo-ha when I was no more than your age, but either I wasn't having any or I was too dense or a combination. I'm not laughing at you, Os, it just cracks me up not hearing that for umpteen years and then you come out with it every night like you're just off the boat."

"That's us," Oskar said. "Swedes. From the old country, like the Professor," he said.

His aunt said, "I won't tell if you won't," and laughed again.

"I have to bless people now."

"I promise not one peep out of me. I think it's sweet." He could feel her fold her hands now, close to his on the cover, thought he could see her bow her head in the darkness this time before he closed his eyes and asked God to bless his mother and father and brother Lars and Aunt Kristina and Aunt Anna, and to help him be good and love all people. She said, "Amen?"

"I have to ask for special helps."

"Scuze me please."

"Please," Oskar said, "help my mom and dad not to have a divorce so I can go home and Lars can go home from visiting Aunt Anna and everything works out fine."

"Ossie, I think that's so nice."

"And please make Mrs. Berntsson stop calling me names when the Professor takes a nap after we eat."

"Dearie," his aunt said, "she can't help it. She's senile. She's probably terrified they'll stick her in a home or she'll die or both."

"Really?"

"It happens when you get real old, knock on wood," she said.

"I'm not done. Please God help the Professor finish his picture of himself."

"Oskar, that is so sweet of you."

"And please help Hank Berntsson not be so nervous from the war so he can get a job and get married with my Aunt

Kristina." He heard something, but did not realize for a moment she had begun to cry.

"And please let Elsa Berntsson and Gene Berntsson like it so they won't try to stop them getting married to live happy ever after." Then he knew she was crying. He tried to think of things to say to help her stop. "How's come Gene Berntsson's so funny? Funny strange I mean." She stopped crying at once, laughed, hiccuped, put her wet cheek next to his. "Isn't he funny strange?"

She laughed, said, "Do you know what a pansy is? Your old man's the one to tell you about that." He said nothing more, lay there with his aunt's head beside his on the pillow, her arms holding him lightly. He closed his eyes again, felt her damp cheek, the movement and sound of her breathing. They lay together like that for a time, and then she got up and went away to her bedroom, and Oskar fell asleep.

Oskar whispered, "Can I ask you a question?"

"Of course. What's the matter?" The Professor's voice was loud in the room, restored by his nap.

"I don't want her to hear me." The Professor looked at his wife.

"She's asleep," he said. "She's tired. We're all tired. Pretty soon, the folks get home, we'll maybe have a little party, huh? What's the question?"

"Does she have to talk mean to me when you take a nap?" Oskar said, afraid to raise his voice. Mrs. Berntsson slept with her eyes partially open, glassy slits catching the last dull light of late afternoon. The Professor cleared his throat loudly before he spoke.

"She can't help that. Kris told you? It's a sickness, you have to ignore things like that."

"It's hard."

"Sure it's hard." Professor Berntsson looked at his sleeping wife, then away from her. "Everything's hard. Life is hard. You better get used to that. Keep your mind on your business, otherwise all you do is worry how hard everything is." He looked at his unfinished painting on the easel, colors indistinct now in the fading light. He laughed a very small laugh.

They sat together in silence on the sofa, waiting for Oskar's aunt and the Professor's children to come home. It felt to Oskar like they sat for a very long time without speaking. Then he said, "If my mom and dad don't have a divorce, I can probably go home tomorrow if they call up on the telephone and tell my Aunt Kristina."

"That's what Kris tells me." It was almost dark in the room now, but they did not turn on the lights.

"But if they have a divorce I don't know what happens then." When the Professor did not speak, he said, "Do you think my mom and dad will have a divorce or stay married?"

"You have to learn to be patient. Patience is a virtue. Things you don't understand, later, if you're lucky you understand things, it all can make sense."

"Do you think Hank and my Aunt Kristina will get married with each other?"

"That's another question. You said one. Anyway, it's complicated," the Professor said.

"How come?"

"People," the Professor said, "have opinions. Opinions, you understand? Some people don't think it's such a good idea."

"Elsa and Gene don't want them to," Oskar said.

He said, "I don't try to understand why people have opinions. It's hard enough to paint pictures." He looked at his pocket watch. "Time Hjalmar and everyone should be home. Who knows," he said, and laughed loudly, "maybe my son got a good job today, he can afford to marry and move to China, whatever he damn wants." Oskar was going to ask if Hank Berntsson might really take his aunt to China if they married, but Mrs. Berntsson woke up.

"Isn't he a pretty boy?" she said. The Professor got up, went to her.

"Hello, Karin," he said, "did you have a good sleep?

Karin, let's go to the bathroom, pretty soon folks get home, we'll forget your worries, have a party, will you like that?"

Oskar waited. He got up and turned on the lights, sat again, looked at the painting, the easel, the pictures hung on the walls, his reflection in the large mirror, waiting for the party they might have when everyone got home.

They thought he was still asleep, but Oskar woke when Hank Berntsson laid him on the cot in his aunt's apartment. He felt the constant tremor that ran through Hank Berntsson's arms as he lowered him to the cot, waking to that unceasing shiver, opening his eyes just enough to see they had not turned the lights on to avoid waking him.

He pretended sleep while his Aunt Kristina slowly undressed him where he lay, covered him with a single, light blanket. "Poor guy, he's dead to the world," she said. He felt her pat the blanket once. They moved away from his cot, and when he heard the sound of their shoes on the tiles in the vestibule, he turned his head toward them, opened his eyes enough to see them, listened.

The corridor's light fell through the open door, silhouetted his aunt and Hank Berntsson, his aunt moving to him, the sound of her spike heels on the hard tile, putting her arms around his neck, their heads touching, the wet smack sound of their kiss. "Stay a while," his aunt said. "I'll build us a drinkie. We can talk in the kitchen. He won't wake for the last trumpet. Please?" She kissed Hank Berntsson again, a long, quiet kiss, the silhouette of her head rolling slowly with his.

Hank Berntsson moved away from his aunt. Oskar saw the shuddering of his head as he spoke. "I better not, Kris. I don't need another drink," and, "I need to get an early start in the morning."

"Take a day off tomorrow," she said. "Come keep Krissie company for a little bit. Pretty please?" She rose to her toes, put her arms around his neck again. Hank Berntsson moved his head away from hers.

"No," he said. "You know Papa expects me to get out every day. If I'm not out wearing out my shoe leather he'll get so upset he won't even be able to paint, I'll hear about it from Elsa and Gene until I'm blue in the face." The catch in his voice became a stammer as he talked.

"Pretty please," Oskar's aunt said, and, "Stay. I'll skip work tomorrow, we can spend the day out, nobody will ever know. Stay," she said. "You can stay here all night with me if we want, Hank."

"No," he said, and removed her hands from around his neck. "Elsa's waiting up for me to get back." He stepped back, the corridor light falling between them, two silhouettes. When his aunt spoke, Oskar caught his breath, held it, pinched his eyelids shut.

"The hell with goddamn Elsa waiting up!"

"You'll wake him."

"The hell with all this crap! I give a good goddamn!"

"Kris—" Hank Berntsson tried to say. Oskar opened his eyes, saw his Aunt Kristina, hands raised, clenched into fists, Hank Berntsson in the doorway to the corridor, head, body, shaking.

"What the hell is this?" she said. "Are we going to get married or is this a goddamn game I'm playing? What the hell should I care what your goddamn old maid sister does or doesn't!" She started to cry.

"I suppose it's my fault I'm sick," he said, stuttered, choked between the words. "Papa's so old," he said. "Elsa wants Mama in a nursing home. Who pays for it all if I don't get well and work? Elsa and Gene carry everything. I can't just say I'm getting married at my age and walk away from everything." He choked so hard he had to stop speaking.

"So go," his aunt said through her crying. "Get your ass to goddamn hell back to your old man and your crazy old lady, Elsa, and your faggy brother!" She closed the door after Hank Berntsson without slamming it, walked quickly through the dark past Oskar's cot to her bedroom, weeping softly.

Oskar held himself as still as if he were dead. He said his prayers to himself without folding his hands, said amen, then asked God to bless his aunt and Hank Berntsson and everyone he knew and everyone else in the world, and then prayed and prayed again the Lord's Prayer in Swedish to himself, until the words became nonsense, dizzying him, until he fell asleep.

They played pinochle. Hank Berntsson moved the Professor's easel to make room for the card table and chairs in the middle of the room. Gene Berntsson brought a teacart with bottles of whiskey and glasses with little knitted coasters fitted to the bottoms, mixed highballs for everyone. "Papa, will you partake of a snort?" he said, and to Oskar, "I have cola and some uncarbonated orange that must surely be prewar if it's a day," and Oskar chose the orange. Elsa Berntsson and Oskar's aunt fixed bowls of snacks, peanuts and chips and some tiny chocolate-covered mints Gene Berntsson said were exquisite if you dissolved them on your tongue with a highball.

"Have you been doing me proud today?" his Aunt Kristina asked him.

"Are you learning to draw from Papa?" Elsa Berntsson said, and, "None of us inherited a lick of all his talent." Oskar asked Hank Berntsson if he had found a job today, and Hank said no such luck.

"Confess," Gene Berntsson said, "did you *look* for work or did you just look for work, Hankie?"

Hank said, "That's a cold world out there," with a little pause between each word.

"You're telling *me* it's a cruel world?" Elsa Berntsson said.

"We can't do more than give it the old college try, can we, darling," Oskar's Aunt Kristina said, and patted the back of Hank's hand.

"Is this pinochle I'm kibitzing or just a gang of Swedes want to gossip all night?" the Professor said. Hank Berntsson and his aunt were partners against Elsa and Gene. The Professor sat on his painting stool, high enough above them all to see their hands and kibitz the tricks they won and lost. Oskar sat on the sofa, drinking uncarbonated orange soda. He watched them all at their game, could see them all, could see himself in the Professor's mirror, the easel and the canvas, covered with a cloth now. He could see Mrs. Berntsson, wrapped in her afghan, watching him and everyone playing pinochle. They slapped their tricks down on the table. They laughed a lot with each trick taken, kept the score on a pad. Between hands, Gene Berntsson got up and mixed more drinks at the teacart. They played and drank highballs and ate snacks. The Professor kibitzed on his stool. Hank Berntsson's fanned cards quivered in his hands. Oskar's aunt moved her chair close to his, patted his arm or hand or shoulder often, leaned over to give him little kisses on the cheek when they took a trick or a hand. Mrs. Berntsson never answered anyone who spoke to her.

"You wouldn't believe these cards she's giving me, Mama," Elsa said.

"Did you have a pleasant day today, Mama?" Gene said, and his father said yes, Karin had a nice day today.

"How are you holding out, doll-boy?" his aunt said to Oskar, and, "Just put your feet up and snooze if you want." He drank the last of his soda, went to the bathroom, then fell asleep on the sofa while they laughed and drank and talked and played pinochle.

Everyone was shouting when he woke. His aunt was crying, and Elsa Berntsson had tears in her eyes, shouting at his aunt. He was suddenly wide awake. They stood up and shouted, then sat back down again. The highball glasses were empty and all the snacks were gone. Mrs. Berntsson was not there, taken to bed while he slept. Oskar pretended he was still sleeping. The Professor sat on his painting stool. When he tried to talk somebody was always up, shouting, so nobody listened to him.

Elsa said, "Gene has his responsibilities and I have mine, and Hank has to take care of his like the rest of us!"

"Who the hell appointed you to tell people's responsibilities!" his aunt shouted back at her. When she stood up and spoke, Elsa Berntsson sat down. His aunt sat down and took hold of Hank Berntsson's arm with both hands. Hank moved his lips, but no words came out.

Gene Berntsson said, "Kris, what Elsa means is we have a situation with Mama and Papa, we have to do what has to be done."

The Professor started to say something, but Oskar's aunt let go her hold of Hank, stood up, and shouted, "We're two adults, we can damn well get married or shack up or run off to Timbuktu if we damn well feel like it!"

When she sat down, Elsa said, "That's lovely language."

"I'll use any damn language I please!" his aunt yelled without getting up, then began to cry harder.

Gene said, "We're only saying you don't understand our situation. We can't just keep Mama here until she rots, can we? And Papa," he said, and the Professor tried to say something, but they did not hear, "Papa," Gene said, "he's old, he'll need the same care. Who's going to provide it if we don't? We need Hank's help, Kristina."

"I can't even help myself," Hank Berntsson said, choking, shaking.

"So where the hell does good old Kris come in?" Oskar's aunt stood up to say. "Old Kris holds her breath until everybody conveniently croaks, is that it?"

"You've lived your life without a husband this long," Elsa said. "What's the mad rush? Maybe my brother's just convenient right now. Is that it?" His aunt was crying too hard to answer her.

Gene said, "It does strike me a little silly. The both of you can hardly be said to be spring chickens. I frankly don't fathom all this passion."

"See, Kris, I told you," Hank Berntsson managed to say, "we're too damn old for this."

Then they were done shouting. His Aunt Kristina cried

harder and harder, until Gene Berntsson gave her his hand-kerchief, and the Professor got off his stool and went to her, put his arm around her, and then Oskar could hear what he said because everyone else was quiet now. "Come on, Kris," Professor Berntsson said, "I'll help you, come wash your face, you'll feel better. We have no business talking about all this after drinking. We should be ashamed. We're all so tired. Just look how your nephew sleeps."

When she came back from the bathroom he pretended to wake. "I fell asleep a long time ago," Oskar said. His aunt, trying to smile at him with her weepy eyes, said it was time to get up and go.

"I don't even remember when I fell asleep," he said. The Professor stood beside his aunt, smiling at Oskar. Elsa Berntsson was very busy, cleaning up the card table. Gene Berntsson mixed himself another highball and said he knew every time he would regret the last one in the cold light of morning. Hank Berntsson sat at the card table while his sister wiped away the crumbs and ashes and drink spills. He sat with his arms folded in front of him, body quivering, muscles in his forearms flexing, a tic flickering along his jaw. Oskar blinked and rubbed his eyes as though he was still too sleepy to see well.

"Goodnight, Professor," he said. "I'll see you in the morning unless I get to go home tomorrow."

"The hell with tomorrow and the whole damn shooting match," his aunt said, taking his hand, pulling him after her to the door. The Professor said goodnight. Elsa Berntsson continued to move about the room, picking up ashtrays to empty. Gene toasted Oskar with his highball, winked. Hank moved his lips, but could not speak.

His aunt said, "Say your prayers if you have to, but say them to yourself." Oskar undressed. His aunt went to the kitchen to make herself a nightcap highball. He listened to her talking to herself. She said, "Shit!" and, "The goddamn hell!" and he heard her light a cigarette, the sound of ice in her glass as she drank. He had his pajamas on when the telephone rang. She came in from the kitchen carrying her drink and cigarette and said, "Beg, damn you, you beg for a change. How's that for the old switcheroo," before she picked up the receiver and said hello very loudly.

Then she said, "Would you mind saving the guff for somebody wants to hear it?" and, "If you don't like the hours I keep you can tell his mother to farm him out to someplace else when she gets in a fight," and, "Look, Annie, do you have something to say to me or do you want to talk to the kid or what?" and, "None of your damn business," and then she began to cry again. She took the receiver from her ear, held it out to Oskar. He put it to his ear, waited for his Aunt Anna to speak.

He watched his aunt find an ashtray for her cigarette, a coaster for her glass, sit on the small chair beside the telephone table. She continued to cry, so he looked away. There was no voice on the phone, just the unbroken whispering sound of the long-distance circuit and his aunt's crying. Then she stopped crying so hard, wiped at her eyes with the back of her hand, took a drink.

"Hello?" Oskar said.

"Oskar? Is that you?" his Aunt Anna said.

"Hi, Aunt Anna," he said. "I'm fine; how are you?"

"Where were you this evening, Oskar?"

"We had a party real late." He looked at his aunt, who laughed and blew her nose into a hankie. She lit a new cigarette, crossed one leg over the other, began to bounce it. She took a long drink from her drink, smoked, tipped her head back to blow the smoke up at the ceiling.

"I can well imagine," his Aunt Anna said, and, "When it rains it pours." Looking at his Aunt Kristina in the chair so near him, listening to his Aunt Anna's voice, he tried but could not imagine how she looked, if she sat or stood as she talked, her face or hair or hands, what room or house she was in as she spoke. Her voice sounded different, as if he heard her on a radio program. "Here's your mother, Oskar," she said.

"Oskar?"

"Hi, I'm fine. I'm being real good," he said. "We had a party and now I'm going to bed." He could not imagine exactly what his mother looked like. He wondered if she had been close by all the time or just now came to the telephone. His Aunt Kristina laughed again, shook her head, like it was the only way she could stop laughing and crying.

"Listen to me," his mother said. "You're to come home tomorrow. I don't know what's going on there, but you tell Kristina you're to be put on the train just as soon as possible tomorrow. Do you hear me?"

"Okay," he said. "I'll show you how I learned to do real good drawing from the Professor. He's real neat. He's Swedes, just like us. He was even born there," and, "Can I say hi to Dad too?" There was a short silence on the telephone. His Aunt Kristina held her drink in one hand, a new cigarette in the other. She was not laughing or crying.

"Would you like to say hello to your brother?" his mother said. He said sure, and almost at once Lars was on the telephone. Oskar tried to imagine them all there, close to the telephone, even his father.

"You sure must of been out late someplace," his brother said.

"Hi," Oskar said. "A party. Are you home already from Aunt Anna's?"

"Where else would I be talking to you from? Don't be dumb," Lars said.

"I'm coming home tomorrow, I guess," he said, but it was his Aunt Anna who answered him. He tried a last time to see them all there by their telephone.

"Let me speak to Kristina at once."

"Can I say hello to Dad first?"

"We'll talk about that when you're back where you belong," she said. He said good-bye and held the receiver out to his Aunt Kristina.

She stood up and laughed and said, "Jump in bed and cover up your head, Os, the air's going to burn around here shortly." He pulled the covers over his head, but still heard what she said. She was still talking, not so loud, when he fell asleep that way, forgetting to pray because he concentrated on listening and trying to think what was said to her to make her say what she did, trying to see all the other people, how they looked, wondering still if there was a chance his father was there with them by their telephone.

Professor Berntsson sat on his stool at the easel, but did not work. The unfinished canvas was still covered with the cloth. He had not opened his tubes of paint, mixed nothing on the palette. Oskar watched the Professor and the image of the Professor and the covered easel and himself on the sofa reflected in the large mirror. Mrs. Berntsson sat in her afghan across the room, smiling, not speaking. "How's come you don't paint any?" he said.

"What's the good?"

"You're almost done."

"Sure," the Professor said, and moved his hands up to cover his face.

"I'm going home today," Oskar said. "When my Aunt Kristina comes home from work we have to go right to the train station. My mom and Aunt Anna said. My brother Lars is already home. Him and my Aunt Anna went home already."

The Professor said nothing, sitting on the stool with his face hidden in his hands. Then he said, "You told me. Kris told me." His voice, muffled by his hands, sounded like he was talking to Oskar long-distance over the telephone.

Oskar looked at Mrs. Berntsson. She smiled harder at him. He looked quickly back at the Professor and said, "I think my mom and dad are having a divorce. I think my dad's already gone away. It didn't all work out in the end," he said, and, "I don't know if it makes sense," and, "My Aunt Kristina says it serves him right." When Professor Berntsson did not speak, he said, "My Aunt Kristina's mad at my mom and my Aunt Anna. I think she's even mad at me, and I didn't even do anything. I behaved . . ." he began to say, then saw the Professor had begun to cry almost silently into his hands. His shoulders moved up and down with his weeping, hunched on the stool.

"Don't," Oskar said. He had never seen a very old person cry. He had cried a lot, and his brother cried a lot before he was thirteen, and his mother and both his aunts. His mother cried when she showed him a picture of his dead Uncle Knute and told him his Uncle Knute was her brother and had been dead a long time and Oskar would never know him. He believed his father must have cried when he was a little boy once. "Don't," Oskar said.

"Oh!" Professor Berntsson said, and then stopped, took his hands away from his face, took off his glasses to dry his eyes, tried to laugh, said *Oh* again.

"Is it funny funny or funny strange?" Oskar said.

"Sure," he said. "Damn funny. Live all your life, and then Karin they put away to die, my daughter tells me what I must do like I'm a child, my sons . . ." he said, but could not finish what he meant to say.

"Hank's not getting married with my Aunt Kristina," Oskar said.

"Sure," he said, and "Hjalmar, Eugene," and then he started to cry again, covered his face. Oskar got up, stood next to him, patted his shaking shoulder. *Oh Oh Oh* the Professor moaned. Oskar looked at Mrs. Berntsson, who was still smiling at them.

"Maybe you could stop and you could paint on your painting and I can do some more drawings," Oskar said. "I think it's real neat doing drawings and paintings all the time. Thanks a lot for teaching me how to do drawing," he said. "When I get home I'll show my mom and Lars and my dad if he's still there how I learned how to do neat drawing."

Mrs. Berntsson began to speak, saying wasn't he a lovely boy, wasn't he a sweet boy, but Oskar did not listen to her. He kept his hand on the Professor's shoulder and thought of all the drawings he would do when he got home.

He made himself try to imagine all the people, their faces, he could draw. He did not listen to her or the Professor. He made himself see all the pictures he would make, all the people he knew. He imagined them all, and then he made himself think how he would ask God to bless each one by name, every night, after he said the Lord's Prayer in Swedish. He would make himself remember all the names until he made pictures of everyone he knew. He would draw pictures of everything, and then he would never forget anything. He could always hold a picture up to the light and remember anything he wanted, and then he would understand it all.

The Interpreter

Words cannot endure,
Petals on summer flowers
Withered by autumn.
       —Basho

It is as if . . .

    It is as if I cannot remember the things I must say to myself. It is as if all the words I know, in both English and my native Mandarin, have fled from me, evaporated into the cold, misty air of this wretched place, into the wet fogs that greet us each morning with the bugle that wakes the camp to another tedious day.

    It is as if each bitter day is the first, and I wake, chilled, huddling on my pallet, knowing nothing until I can remember some words, something to say to myself that will allow me to rise, answer the bugle's summons, stand in formation in the compound, call roll in the sharp glint of daybreak's cold, eat, take up the routine of my duty . . . It is as if there is nothing, no shape, texture, no sense, unless and until I find some words that will enable me to begin again.

I wake to the piercing bugle, and there are no longer even dreams to remember, to know that I have been sleeping. Surely I dream when I sleep! But I do not, cannot remember my dreams, and I am only awake in the dark of my hut, wrapped, huddling against the terrible cold, and there is nothing except the dark cold. Until I find words.

It is necessary to think to myself: I am Li; I am a soldier of the heroic Chinese Volunteer Army; I participate in the valiant struggle to liberate this wretched place, to repel the aggression of Yankee imperialists and their running dog henchmen of the so-called Republic of Korea; it is dark, and I am cold, and the strident bugle calls us to formation in the bleak, windswept compound, and I must rise from my pallet, go to call the roll, begin another day . . .

I think: I am Li. I am a Probationary Graduate of the People's Institute for Study of Alien Languages. I am far from my country, from my native city of Hangkow, from my parents, brothers, sisters. I am called upon to abandon my study of English language and literature for the duration of our valiant struggle against Yankee Imperialism. I am an enthusiastic soldier in the ranks of the heroic Chinese Volunteer Army. I am here in this wretched place called Prisoner Compound Number Nineteen, in a fog-drenched valley surrounded by ragged mountains, near a filthy village called Yong Dong Po, now deserted, the villagers driven away by the war, our presence here.

I am awake, listening to the bugle's shriek that comes out of the frozen dark. And then I hear my clerk, Comrade Volunteer Ma, as he stirs, rises from his dirty pallet in the black cold of this hut we share. He coughs, clears his throat.

"The bugle," mumbles Comrade Volunteer Ma, and coughs.

"I hear the bugle, Comrade Ma," I say, and, "Do not dare to spit on the floor. If you spit on the floor, ever again, I shall report you to the camp commandant, and you will be punished and returned to the ranks of those who escort the prisoners to work in the fields! Another man who can read and write will be found to take your place if you do not learn to refrain from spitting on the floor, Ma!"

The bugle ceases, and there is silence for a moment—only the darkness and the unceasing cold. And then Comrade Volunteer Ma, my clerk, says, "I try to remember not to spit, Comrade Interpreter."

"Light the candle, Ma," I say to him. "Another day begins."

Comrade Guard-Escort Hong trembles. It is necessary to say something to put him at his ease if we are to resolve this. I say to him, "Comrade Guard Hong, relax your belly, and then we may speak to some point here."

"My belly is not nervous, Comrade Interpreter," Hong says. This is an impudence, but I choose to ignore that; I am accustomed to the impudence of ignorant men—it is, I have concluded, only the expression of their fear and awe of the educated—and so try never to respond in anger.

"Then if your belly is not nervous, you are able to stand at attention, are you not, Comrade Guard-Escort Hong? We may not behave casually in this, as I have told you so often before." Hong ceases to tremble.

Prisoner Lester Boggs also trembles, shudders, and twitches, picks at his trouser legs with his grimy nail-bitten fingers, shuffles his feet. He, of course, fears punishment, the wheel and the pit.

When it is time to speak in English, as it is now, I remind myself to speak slowly, to exaggerate my pronunciation, to watch the prisoner's face closely for any slightest expression of mockery or silent contempt.

I say to Prisoner Lester Boggs, Private, Army of the United States, "Prisoner Boggs, does heart flutters prevent to stand at correct postures of attention whilst conduct of official procedures proceeds?"

It is a thing I alone in this wretched place, the sole Chinese speaker of English here, know: in our Mandarin, we speak of the stomach as the center of one's being, where reside both the base emotions and nobler sentiments; in English—this I know from my incompleted studies at the People's Institute for Study of Alien Languages—we speak of course of the heart. Witness J. Conrad's *Heart of Darkness*, or Mr. Hawthorne's marble heart, or the folksong entitled "My Heart's in the Highlands," which emanates from the decadent royalist United Kingdom—examples are myriad in both the popular and sophisticated literatures of the English-speaking cultures.

"Huh?" grunts Prisoner Lester Boggs.

Does he feign, or has he truly not understood my words? Indecision is unacceptable; I must act, always, decisively—as though, even if the matter is as inscrutable as the long black winter nights in this wretched place, the light of my articulation shows brightly into every corner, and my action is as coherent as the terms that pronounce it.

"Stand attention!" I shout at Prisoner Lester Boggs—so loud is my voice that Ma, my clerk, who dozes on his chair at the small table that holds the ledger, snaps awake, eyes suddenly wide and alert, and the pen falls from his fingers to the packed-earth floor of the hut; Comrade Guard-Escort Hong dares to smile—another impudence—as Prisoner Lester Boggs brings himself to a more correct posture. Yet he continues to shiver where he stands, chattering his broken, yellow teeth. "Stand attention!" I repeat, and, "Can you not stop to shake, Prisoner Boggs? Perhaps it is fear of merited retributions than which so inspires involuntary motion, hence betraying guilt my charge is to discern?"

"Huh?" says Prisoner Lester Boggs, and, "It's cold in here, Comrade!" and, "I been froze hard as a carp since roll call standing out in the damn wind all morning before now, man!"

"Cease to speak!" I command him; I must not permit the prisoner to confuse our purpose here with talk of the cold, and

I must make the impudent smirk disappear from the face of Comrade Hong. "State the nature of the complaint you bring to me against this prisoner, Comrade!" I say to him. Ma has retrieved his pen from the dirt floor, holds it, poised above the ledger's page for this day, prepared to make the entry.

"The same thing as always with him," Guard-Escort Hong says, and, "The same as always with all of the devils, no matter if they are white or dark." He continues to smirk at me, as though I were a child who has forgotten his lesson, must be coached into memory with mockery.

"Do not write until I tell you to do so," I tell Ma before he can begin to mar the ledger page with his scarcely legible calligraphy. To this impudent Hong I say, "If you cannot state your complaint in exact and lucid terms, I shall be pleased to summon an officer who will assist you—even the camp commandant if you wish—and he would, I am certain, also be pleased to ask you why your face betrays levity when the matter at hand is so serious! Would you like me to send the comrade clerk to summon an officer, Comrade Hong?" The infuriating smirk evaporates from his stupid peasant's face, and he stands now at a very correct posture of attention.

"Prisoner Lester Boggs cursed me with vile words in his language," says Guard-Escort Hong.

"Do not yet begin to write!" I say quickly to Ma; for his impudence, I shall prolong this Hong's recitation. It will humiliate him to have to respond to me at greater than usual length; he will, I know, lie to his fellow guard-escorts when they ask him why he was so long in my hut over the matter concerning Prisoner Lester Boggs. To Hong, I say, "Perhaps," and, "Please tell me of the attendant circumstances." There is no smirk on his face now; his eyes narrow as he realizes my intention. "Please, Comrade," I say to him, and I smile.

"We were in the fields, Comrade Interpreter."

"And what were you about while you were in the fields, you and Prisoner Lester Boggs? This was yesterday?"

"Of course."

"I ask only to be certain, for you will of course recall that complaints involving vile language must be reported to me no later than one day after the occurrence. You do remember this from the very first class I taught to instruct you and all your comrades as to required procedures, do you not, Comrade Hong?"

"I remember, Comrade Interpreter."

"And do you also remember the justification for this regulation regarding timely reporting of such incidents?"

"It is so that my comrades and I will not forget the exact sounds of the English words we do not understand, so that we can repeat them to you with accuracy, so that you can decide if they are indeed vile." Prisoner Lester Boggs cannot cease his shivering, but I ignore this, because I would teach this Hong a lesson, as a wise teacher will ignore the lesser mischief of one pupil in order to confront the greater misbehavior of another.

"Excellent! This occurred yesterday, in the fields. I ask again, Comrade Hong, what were you about, you and Prisoner Lester Boggs, there in the fields yesterday?" When he hears his name spoken in the flow of Mandarin that is as incomprehensible to him as if it were a pure darkness his eyes sought to penetrate—like the winter nights in this wretched place—or the intricacy of political dialectic, or a subtle passage in literature, or even some refined locution in his own language, Prisoner Lester Boggs momentarily arrests his spasms, cocks his head at us, as if he listened to and understood all we say.

"As always," Hong says, and, "He dug the turnips from the ground. I stood guard and watched, as it is my duty as a soldier to do."

"And of a sudden, without cause, the prisoner cursed you with vile language?" I smile at Comrade Guard-Escort Hong. His eyes narrow, and I know I have caused great anger in his belly, and so I smile broadly at him as he answers me.

"No. Prisoner Boggs shirked his work. I saw this. His

comrades dug the turnips from the ground. They worked diligently, but this prisoner only pretended to work. He sat on the ground where the turnips grow, but he dug few from their holes, and only pretended to dig deeply to get the turnips."

"This is serious," I say, and I smile only a little. "Write nothing as yet!" I caution Ma. And to Hong, I say, "And what action did you take when you observed the prisoner shirking his work?"

"I ordered him to work, like his comrades."

"What, precisely, did you say to Prisoner Lester Boggs?" In the corner of my eye, at the edge of my vision, I see Prisoner Lester Boggs lean forward upon hearing his name, and I smile.

"I said only, work!"

"Did you say this in English, so that he might understand your command to him?"

"Of course!"

"To be sure," I say, "so that we do not act in haste and thus perhaps make a mistake—which in this matter is to commit an injustice, Comrade Guard-Escort, repeat for me, exactly, what you said to the prisoner yesterday in the fields when you observed that he shirked his work? The exact word or words, Comrade," I say, "just as you spoke, in English, please."

Hong does not speak at once. I see that he clenches his fingers into fists at his side, grips his rifle with his other hand so tightly his knuckles lose their redness; I hear the leather of his cartridge belt creak as he struggles to control the fury I have engendered in his belly. I smile at him, at Prisoner Lester Boggs, at Comrade Ma, who waits with his pen at the small table to write in the ledger.

"Do you tease or shame me, Comrade Interpreter?" Hong says at last.

"Of course not, Comrade!" I say quickly, with a big smile, and, "My concern is only to be certain that what you said—which must be considered the provocation for the prisoner's vile language which you say ensued—was uttered intelligibly by you. For, Comrade, if your pronunciation of the English word or words was such as to be unintelligible to the prisoner, then his response—however vile, however obscene—may not be punished, or at least the punishment decreed must be mitigated if I determine he was unable to understand your command. If he is guilty as you allege, he shall go upon the wheel in the pit, but for a limited duration only if I decide there is mitigation in the circumstance. Do you comprehend my meaning, Comrade Hong?" Again, he does not speak, cannot speak until he has mastered the rage that burns his belly. I do not smile as I wait for him to speak; my expression is patient, indulgent.

Comrade Guard-Escort Hong says at last, "I said to him only the word, *work*, and I said it in English in this way, I said: *work! work! work!* And I pointed with my rifle to the ground where the turnips grow, where he sat, shirking, and I pretended to be digging, as if my rifle were a hoe, and I said to him in his English: *work! work! work!* I know he understood me!"

I hear, so faint that I doubt Hong or Ma can hear it, Prisoner Lester Boggs mutter to himself when he hears the English word Hong repeats so loudly; I hear Prisoner Lester Boggs mutter, "Work my sweet damn ass!" I cannot overlook this.

"Silent at attention, Prisoner Boggs!" I shout, and slap his face—I do not slap him hard, but the sound of it cracks like a whip in the air of my hut, so cold we can see our breath, like the shadows of the words we speak.

Quickly, because I am suddenly weary . . . it is as if the smack of my palm against the prisoner's dirty cheek has opened a hole in me, drained away my strength and my resolve, my purpose . . . quickly, I turn to Guard-Escort Hong.

"I congratulate you on the precision of your pronunciation of this English word, Comrade. No man could have failed to understand you. Now tell me what the prisoner said upon hearing this word. His word or words to you? Come, Comrade," I say, "let us be done with this! You and I have other duties to perform." To Ma, I say, "Write that Prisoner Lester Boggs was observed to shirk his assigned work. Write that the Comrade Guard-Escort ordered him to work. Comrade?" I say to Hong. Comrade Hong looks at me, at the prisoner, at Ma; he is confused.

"Say to me, here in this hut," I say to him, "exactly the English word or words he uttered, and which you sincerely believe to be vile."

Hong says, "The prisoner said to me: *suck cock*." Prisoner Lester Boggs, no longer trembling, listens closely now.

"He said exactly that, *suck cock?*"

"Yes, Comrade Interpreter."

"It was no variant upon this obscenity? He did not say, *suck my cock*, or *you suck cock*, or perhaps he said to you, *you cocksucker?*" Prisoner Boggs grins at us.

"I do not think so. I was careful to memorize exactly what I heard. I believe I heard *suck cock*, Comrade."

"Write this in the ledger," I command Ma, "that Prisoner Lester Boggs did curse his guard-escort with vile language, in that he did say to him, *suck cock*—you know the calligraph I devised for this obscenity, write it."

As I turn to address Prisoner Lester Boggs in English, I see Comrade Hong's smile, hear his sigh; he will lie to his comrades when he tells them of this, because he fears they will mock him for all the questions he was required to answer, but he will take satisfaction in the severe punishment I mete out—wheel and pit—to the prisoner for his serious infraction of the camp's good order and discipline, as codified in the Geneva Convention.

I speak slowly, taking great care with pronunciation, for this is a matter of much gravity. "Prisoner Lester Boggs," I say, "I discern you have gross fashion violated camp's discipline. You did speak Guard-Escort Hong that he suck cock, that which is blatant palpable obsceneness disrespect of duly designated guard-escort in performance of assigned duty. Also you slack work, only fake to dig turnips, thus deprive your comrades of needed nutritious rations. Punishments are merited as I mandate! Has you words of mitigation prior to I pronounce?" Prisoner Boggs coughs, sniffs, wipes his runny nose on the crusty sleeve of his tattered coat.

"You saying I done it, ain't you," Prisoner Boggs says, and, "I knowed as soon as I come in here on report you was fixing to stick it to me, the both of you."

"Irrelevance!" I say, and, "Nothing further of mitigations weighty?"

"I never," says Prisoner Boggs, and, "I never said no such a thing to him! He's just out to stick it to me on account of he knows I hate his ass worse'n a damn black nigger's!"

"Silence whilst at postures of attention!" I shout; my words erupt from my mouth in puffs, like smoke, in the cold air of the hut. To Hong, I say in Mandarin, "You are dismissed, Comrade Hong. Your presence is not required for the pronouncement of punishment. Return to your duties, Comrade."

"He deserves the most severe punishment," this impudent Guard-Escort Hong says, and, "They all do, the white devils and the dark ones even more, for they all mock me and my comrades repeatedly with their nasty words! They will not cease to do this unless you decree the most severe punishments!" he says.

"You are dismissed!" I shout at him, and, "You have performed your duty; now I shall perform mine, and this matter is no longer of concern to you!"

"I will leave," Hong says, "but I beg your permission to ask but one question before I go."

"Ask it quickly."

"What does *suck cock* mean, Comrade Interpreter?"

"The meaning of this locution is also none of your concern, Comrade," I tell him, "for the meaning of words in English is the sole responsibility of the camp interpreter. To me belong both the English words uttered by our prisoners and their respective meanings. I do not presume to escort prisoners when they go to the turnip fields to work, and it is not for you to presume to concern yourself with what words in English may signify. I have answered your question. You are dismissed, Comrade!"

Do I see the trace of a smile on Comrade Guard-Escort Hong's chapped lips as he turns and leaves the hut? No matter— his humiliation has been adequate to its provocation, and by virtue of what I will now do, he will have no cause to complain of me to his comrades when they gossip of this. There is a rush of cutting cold air, a brief glimpse of snowflakes in the gray air of morning outside when Hong opens and shuts the door behind him. I shiver.

"Write this," I say to Ma. "Write that Prisoner Lester Boggs is determined to be guilty of the infraction charged. Write that Prisoner Boggs is notorious for his infractions of the rule of camp's discipline prohibiting the cursing of officers and others in positions of command authority. He thus merits the most severe discipline. Write that I sentence him to twenty-four hours of punishment, this punishment to be effected immediately. Write that Prisoner Lester Boggs, private soldier of the Army of the United States of America, 109th Quartermaster Company, 2d Infantry Division, Eighth Army, prisoner of war in the custody of the heroic Chinese Volunteer Army, Prisoner Compound Number Nineteen, located in the vicinity of the village of Yong Dong Po, in the imperialist's puppet Republic of Korea we seek to liberate, shall be bound to the discarded caisson wheel in the camp's refuse pit, there to remain for twenty-four hours. Date this entry in the ledger for my signature."

"Twenty-four hours, Comrade Interpreter?" says Ma.

"Are your ears clogged with wax that you do not hear me, Ma?" I say, and, "Write what I have said, and when the entry is completed, I shall endorse it with the calligraph of my name.

Do you hear and understand me, Ma? Write!" My clerk, Comrade Volunteer Ma, who is a simple and barely literate peasant, dips his pen in the inkpot, shakes the excess onto the floor, tests the point on his thumb, begins to write his graceless calligraphy.

"Lester Boggs, you do this swearing of dirty words repeated," I say in English.

"I never," Boggs says.

"Repeated!" I say. "My toleration is transgressed. This time wheel and pit for twenty-four hours consecutive. No remission. Think in undignified and painful duration of solitary durance of your sins of dirty swearing at peoples, whoever, as you lie full twenty-four hours amongst camp's garbage and smell it coupled with odor of adjacent latrines, Lester Boggs!"

"Twenty-four hours," Prisoner Boggs says, and then he says nothing, and then he says, "I'll freeze to damn death out there in that shit if you tie me to that wheel all night, Comrade."

"Too tardy to reconsider," I say, and, "Entry even as we speak enters ledger, official rendition, power of fact and law, Geneva Convention, Lester Boggs. You have the dirty mouth, and I strive to maintain maintenance of camp disciplines and good orders whilst arresting your antisocial characteristic. Do you understand and comprehend me, Lester Boggs?"

"Man," is all Prisoner Lester Boggs can say, and then he says, "I'll die if you tie me out there in the garbage that long, man!"

"You will be feeded. Also water. Note I do not interdict rations. I am humanistic, Lester Boggs. Ma, can you not write faster?" I say to my clerk in Mandarin.

"It might could get below zero out there at night," Prisoner Boggs says, and, "It might could snow all night tonight to where I'll be covered up and drownded in snow when they come to turn me loose in the morning. Man, I can't stand this cold!" Ma writes as fast as his numbed fingers permit, dipping his pen in the inkpot, shaking drops on the earthen floor, testing it on his thumb, black with ink. "I growed up in Oklahoma!" Prisoner Lester Boggs says, and he begins to cry. His large eyes fill suddenly with tears; they brim, and tears course down his stubbled, dirty cheeks, gather in the corners of his mouth; his nose runs like a child's, and he begins to rock back and forth on the worn heels of his torn boots. I try to be precise when I speak English!

"Military disciplines!" I say, and, "Act the man, Boggs," and "This is embarrassment mutually," and, "Where now is vaunted Yankee imperialist arrogance?" and, "Please not crying, Boggs!"

"Comrade," he blubbers while Ma writes in the ledger, "I never even should of been here! I am just a good old boy shitkicker, man! I never wanted to soldier, but they made me! I never wanted to leave Stillwater, Oklahoma, Comrade Li! All my life I been messed up! I had just got me a job keeping grounds for the A & M college, and they right away made me go and soldier! Why you doing me this, Comrade? All my damn life, people to home, the damn army, all these damn niggers I got to live with here, and now you're killing me by freezing me to death if you put me out there in the garbage dump all night long, man!" And then he is crying too hard to continue to speak.

Ma, my clerk, pauses in his writing to look at Boggs, at me, to smile. He says, "Look how the prisoner weeps like an infant, Comrade! How shall our heroic Volunteer Army fail to defeat the imperialist Yankees when their soldiers cannot show courage when they face pain and death?"

"Close your mouth!" I shout at Ma, and, "He has not been sentenced to death! He may well survive the twenty-four hours! You are an ignorant peasant, and if you do not learn soon to write so that others may read your words without hesitation and confusion, I shall recommend you be sent to join our valiant comrades who daily face death at the hands of the Yankees, who, even as we talk here, face their terrible cannons and machineguns and bombs from airplanes! We are locked in struggle to liberate this wretched country! We fight People's War to continue the glorious People's Revolution, and you are a stupid and inept clerk," I tell him, "and know nothing of the true courage that distinguishes a man!"

Comrade Ma writes slowly, carefully in the ledger. Prisoner Lester Boggs covers his face with his grimy hands, weeps, shoulders hunched and shaking. His long, knotted red hair quivers, as if a breeze blew here inside my hut.

I think on the virtue of courage, and wonder if I should exhibit it were I to face the Yankee armies in battle, if I were not who and what I am—Li, interpreter of English, here in this wretched place. I wonder if I have true courage, and I think upon the fictions of E. Hemingway which I read as a student at the People's Institute for Study of Alien Languages—I think of grace in the face of adversity, of the ethic which compels the matador to stand fast in the path of the charging bullock, of E. Hemingway's crisp words describing death in wars, and I cannot but conclude that I do not know if I should behave any differently than Prisoner Lester Boggs, who tries to control his weeping.

"Grace under fire, Boggs." I say to him, and, "You will not wish to display before comrade prisoners womanish sentiments, Boggs," and, "Lester, shall you not rather have been example of martial airs for all us who suffer this bad times here? Finish writing!" I say to Ma in Mandarin.

"I know what it is," Lester Boggs says when his tears slow. "You and Hong, all of you, is after sticking it to me because I'm white, isn't it?"

"Boggs," I say, "you speak absurd!"

"Sure thing!" he says, and, "All you damn gooks carrying hard-ons for me and us white boys all of us! You don't never get after the niggers like you do us because you think because we're white folks you got to go easy on niggers because they colored like you! Don't tell me I don't know, man, you give us all that race shit in class, you don't never get after any niggers like you do me! If I was a damn black nigger I wouldn't be getting killed freezing to death for something I never even said even if you say I did!"

"Boggs!" I shout. "Boggs, you speak perfidy! I am humanistic! I am of the complected peoples of the world long oppressed like unto your Negro comrades, racist imperialism victims of decadent West, this we teach in dialectic discussion as Comrade Political Cadre instructs! Do not dare to say I oppress on line of coloration! Marx and Engels prescribe otherwise, Lester Boggs! Do not dare allege I oppress you!"

Prisoner Boggs wipes his eyes and nose and mouth with his hands, wipes his hands on his patched trousers, and now he sneers at me as he speaks. So shocked am I at what he has said, I do not think to order him to resume his stance at attention.

"Bull fucking shit!" Lester Boggs says, and, "I seen it happen!" and, "You let them niggers off when they cuss out the guards, but us white boys gets the purple shaft ever' time, even when we ain't said nothing, no matter what fucking damn Hong lied and said I said!" Ma still writes, slowly, carefully, in the ledger book.

"Prevarication!" I say to Boggs. "Falsehoods! Calumny! Slanders!"

"Smith for one," Boggs says before I can command him to be silent. "How many times that nigger pimp sumbitch been in here and no punishment for calling guards names I ain't never even heard of in Stillwater, Oklahoma, nor no place else I ever been neither? Fucking Smith," Lester Boggs says, "You don't never punish him none, not once, do you, Comrade! Comrade my sweet damn Oklahoma ass!" Boggs says.

"Can you not continue to complete the entry?" I say in Mandarin to Ma while I try to think what to say to Lester Boggs.

"I strive to write legibly, Comrade," Ma says, "but I

am distracted by the din of the English you speak with the prisoner."

"Finish!" I say to him, and to Lester Boggs, searching for the correct words and syntax, "Prisoner Boggs, I am but one sole frail human personage. Not unlike you. Hence brotherhood of men we teach when we assemble with Comrade Political Cadre Soo to discuss dialectic. I do not oppress! I love all men regardless of respect for hues of skin color, Boggs! My task is unenviable. Do you comprehend me, Boggs?" I am not sure he listens, understands what I try to say.

"Lester," I say, "mine the task deciding words of English and respective denotations. I must rely on phoneticisms uttered by comrade guards who report same. Mine the task to maintain maintenance of camp good order and military disciplines. Geneva Convention, Boggs. Codified, right and wrong, do you not see? Wrong to swear at guards, Lester! Punishments mandated."

"So how's come," Lester Boggs says, "it ain't never no wrong when Raleigh Smith and his nigger pals does it?"

"Boggs." I say, and, "Lester." I attempt to think of examples from the noble tradition of letters—I think of Madam H. B. Stowe's Uncle Thomas, Mr. Clemens' Jim, the Harlem argot chronicled by L. Hughes. But I can only say to him, "Lester, be secure I shall punish all with equality, to include Corporal Raleigh Furman Smith, despite attendant hues. Negro or not, if such come to my hut on report for vile speeches, this I vow, Lester!"

"So how's come you don't hardly never?" he asks.

"I am finished, Comrade!" cries Ma as he wipes his pen on his tunic, covers the inkpot, blows on the ledger page to dry his calligraphy.

"It is only," I say to Lester Boggs, "the cases of my failings to recognize words account for this, Lester. Speech," I say, "of English as spoke by Raleigh Furman Smith and Negroid comrades of dim hue is opaque upon my ear. Do you comprehend, Lester? So often, bane of my conduct of assigned duty, I cannot comprehend meanings of words they speak, thus prohibited in the punishment where I fail to discern crime of obscenity. Words uttered by Raleigh Furman Smith," I say to him, "are often most not familiar. I want always to comprehend. What shall a man else have done, Lester," I ask, "when he knows not what is said?"

"You may sign the entry, Comrade Interpreter," Ma says, "while I summon a guard-escort to take the prisoner to the refuse pit."

"Can you not comprehend me, Lester?" I say, wave Ma out the door.

"Shit and fall back in it!" Prisoner Boggs says, and "All's I know is you done killed me by freezing me to death, you damn gook sumbitch!" While we wait for Ma to return with an escort for him, Prisoner Lester Boggs begins to weep again. I can think of nothing to say to him, no words he would understand.

"Perhaps," I say to him as he leaves under escort, "the night shall grow milder warm tonight, Boggs, and what matter shall it have been then?"

I think: I am Li. I am a soldier in the heroic Chinese Volunteer Army. I am called upon to lend my total effort to the struggle for liberation against the oppression of Yankee Imperialism and the capitalist running dogs of the puppet Republic of Korea. This higher purpose has caused me to interrupt my education, to leave the People's Institute for Study of Alien Languages, to come to this wretched place called Yong Dong Po—so far from my home and family in Hangkow city—to serve the cause of People's War and People's Revolution. I know my duty, and I pledge myself to perform it!

I think: I am Li, a lover of words. I love the music of my native Mandarin, love the flow of its play on my tongue, love the precise and intricate shapes of its calligraphy. I, Li, am a lover of words. I love the bite and smack of harsh English in my mouth, the march of its strong alphabet, the inexorable logic of grammar, the closed, symmetrical beauty of story and poem.

I think: Li, in your brain contend the forces of two languages—so different, so disparate, so utterly alien!—and it is your task in life to order this chaos, to sort this clash of sound and shape and sense, to create by the alchemy of translation the meaning and meanings by which men—the Spirit of Man!—may come to that condition of higher existence, that fruition of spirit which is the true goal of all moral endeavor!

This, I think—my struggle with the clashing words of my two languages—is how I, Li, participate nobly and with dignity in the causes of People's War and People's Revolution! All else—duty, dialectic, the sordid routine of days and nights in this wretched place—all else is but a twisting, mundane path I must trod, step by step, like the words of a long English sentence, if I am to serve what I love. I do not flinch in the face of my journey's adversities. I am Li, I think, a true lover, and in my faithfulness to my love lies my courage!

I think: Li, if this night to come is cold enough, Prisoner Lester Boggs will freeze to death in the refuse pit. Lester Boggs will die for the words he spoke, and I, Li, shall have been the instrument of his execution. Li, I think, because you so love your words, you shall be thought by some to be a murderer . . . is it moral, I ask myself, for a man to love that which kills another? Shall the death of Lester Boggs serve the causes of the People's War and People's Revolution? Ah, Li! I think: be humble! Tremble—as Boggs, as all of us here in Prisoner Compound Number Nineteen, close to the deserted village of Yong Dong Po, tremble in the winter's cold—tremble, Li, as you contemplate the awful power of the words you so love! Be humble, Li, and be courageous!

Comrade Ma, my clerk, cleans his pens—wipes them on his ink-spotted tunic, licks the points with his blackened tongue, wipes them dry, arranges them neatly beside the ledger book on the small table. "Will you affix your signature to the entry, Comrade Interpreter?" he asks.

I look up, pretend to have been absorbed in the study of one of my English glossaries, stare at him with an abstracted expression before I speak. "In a moment," I say, and, "Did you observe Prisoner Boggs as he was taken to the refuse pit?"

"I did, Comrade."

"Did he resist? Did he show courage? Was he still weeping as they took him?"

"He did not resist. I could not see if he wept or not, Comrade. I heard him call out to his comrades who stood in ranks in the compound. He shouted to them, but of course I do not know what words he said. His comrades jeered and shouted more words I do not know, and then the guard-escorts began to blow their whistles to call the prisoners to order, and they began to march them out of the compound to work in the fields."

"I heard the shouting and the whistles," I say to Ma, and, "How does the sky look to you, Ma? Will there be a storm tonight? You are a peasant, you are supposed to be able to read the coming weather in the sky, what do you predict?"

Ma smiles; the decaying, broken teeth in his mouth remind me of Lester Boggs's. "I cannot say, Comrade," he says, and, "My father was reputed to be able to read the coming weather in the look of the sky and the noise of insects, but I do not think he could. I remember once that he said it would surely rain, so our commune must be quick to harvest the rice in the paddies, but I remember that it did not rain, and our commune's political cadre mocked my father, and called him a decadent fool, and he was disgraced for a long time in our commune. I only know it is cold outside today, Comrade, with a little snow in the wind, and are not the nights always colder than the days, in all seasons?" When I do not speak, he says, "Will you sign the ledger now, Comrade?"

"Comrade Ma," I say, "I have two tasks for you to perform. Go, now, to the guard posted at the compound gate. Tell him to send a runner to the fields. Have the prisoner, Corporal Raleigh Furman Smith, the Negro, brought to me here as soon as possible. Do you understand? Do this first. Then go to the refuse pit and look at Lester Boggs. Observe his demeanor. Listen to anything he may say, try to remember the sound of it, and come quickly back here and repeat it to me. Do you understand these tasks, Ma?"

"I have no ear for remembering the sounds of English words, Comrade."

"This I know, Ma! Try!"

"I will try, Comrade, but there is so much to remember! I must remember not to spit on the floor. I must remember to write slowly so that my calligraphy is legible to all!" Then he repeats the name for me: *Raleigh Furman Smith.*

"Well done, Ma," I say, and, "I have confidence in you, Comrade," and, "There will be no confusion as to who to send to me from the fields if you say it just so. Go now, at once," I tell him, "and I will have signed your ledger entry before you reach the compound gate."

It is as if . . . as if I stood alone in some vast darkness. There is no sound to be heard in this darkness; or perhaps there is the sound of a wind that whips and twists through the impenetrable dark. And it is cold. Yes, it is as if it were this wretched place, except that there is no Prisoner Compound Number Nineteen, no nearby deserted village of Yong Dong Po, no prisoners, no comrades of the Chinese Volunteer Army; there is only the cold and wind of a severe winter. I, Li, stand alone in this dark, and am unable to speak. No words of my lovely Mandarin come to me, no stalwart words of English. I am alone in this cold, windy dark, and shall remain here until I can find words to say. If I can find words, speak, give voice to them, then perhaps I will escape this black solitude, but there seem to be no words, nothing I can think of to say to save myself.

Corporal Raleigh Furman Smith is such a man as I might—in another life, if I were not destined to be who and what I am—have wished to be. He is tall, slender, his eyes bright with intelligence, his skin scarcely darker than mine. He is a man of quick wit and quicker speech, and though uneducated, an instinctive leader among his Negro comrade prisoners. They were all taken together—Lester Boggs and his fellow Caucasians, Raleigh Furman Smith and his Negro comrades—by our swiftly advancing Volunteer Army, during the victorious push south from the Chosin Reservoir, just after we crossed the Yalu to liberate this wretched place from their grasp. They are a gang of stragglers and shirkers, poor soldiers, conscripts of the 109th Quartermaster Company of the 2d Infantry Division who surrendered without resistance to our heroic Volunteers. They are a sorry lot, the dregs of a corrupt bourgeoise society, and it is only natural that I should hold them in contempt. We have had them in our custody a full year in this wretched place, and all our patient efforts to rehabilitate them with the tonic of dialectic are to no avail.

But I continually remind myself that despair is unacceptable in the light of the historical necessity we learn from masters Marx and Engels, from Comrades Lenin and Stalin, Mao and Chou, and our great teacher of People's War, Lin Piao. And when I look upon Corporal Raleigh Furman Smith, I am reminded of the dialectic which teaches that the oppressed masses will always engender a cadre of leadership which, guided by the light of historical and materialistic dialectics, has the power to lift those masses out of their degradation and oppression. The fish in the sea, Lin Piao has written, may be nurtured to become sharks. And have not U. Sinclair and J. Steinbeck and others dramatized the resurgent capacity of the lowly masses to create the terms of their salvation?

"Prisoner Corporal Raleigh Furman Smith," I say as he stands before me in my hut, "welcome to my domicile, Comrade Prisoner! At ease please. I summon you from your duty in turnip fields for informal confabulations only, no implications of officialdom pertains."

"Say what?" says Prisoner Raleigh Furman Smith.

I am careful to smile, to in no way betray my consternation before Ma—though Ma nods, half-asleep at his table— and Guard-Escort Hong, who has, impudently, taken it upon himself to personally bring the prisoner back to the compound from the fields; Comrade Hong is curious, and I will not satisfy his curiosity, and I will not allow either Hong or Ma to suspect the enormous difficulty of communication I always experience when I speak with Raleigh Furman Smith.

"I think, Raleigh Smith," I say, "you comprehend me even when you profess contrary, is this not correct?" and, "I wish to speak concerning disposition of punishments accorded Prisoner Lester Boggs. Thereof are you cognizant, Raleigh Smith?" When he hears the name of Lester Boggs, Raleigh Smith's countenance alters; his habitual frown of defiant petulance dissolves into a wicked leer, and he relaxes his casual posture of attention, places his hands on his hips, leans back, one booted foot thrust forward.

"Ain't this a bitch!" says Corporal Raleigh Furman Smith, and, "I hear talk as how you done fixed his cracker ass to that wheel for all day *and* night, freeze the mother's ass solid, Jim! It's time somebody killed the little mother, save me or somebody the doing," says Prisoner Smith.

I say in Mandarin to Hong, "You have done as I requested, Comrade. I prefer that you wait elsewhere while I speak with the prisoner."

"It is very cold outside in the wind, Comrade Interpreter," Hong says, and, "What does it matter if I wait in the shelter of your hut when I cannot understand what you say to him, or he to you?"

"Nevertheless," I say to him, "you are dismissed!"

"It is irregular to summon a prisoner from work when there has been no report of his misconduct made to you. I am justified in bringing this to the attention of the Comrade Camp Commandant," he says.

"Dismissed!" I order him, and he leaves, smiling impudently at me before he closes the door.

"Gabble gabble, people steady talking shit about me I can't understand no more than if it was some damn animal noises," Raleigh Smith says.

"If you are persisting in vulgarisms," I say to him, "we shall fail communications. Prisoner Smith, please not to pollute discourse with such as shit and ass, please! Such words are forbidden by Geneva Convention and also offensive to ears of all parties."

"Not his it ain't," Smith says, turns to look at dozing Ma. "That ugly cat don't dig no more what I say than I do that turkey-gabble you steady talking around me, Jim."

"Ma, either rouse yourself to a semblance of consciousness or join Comrade Hong outside in the wind and snow!"

"Forgive me, Comrade," Ma says, "but I think the cold weather makes me sleepy. Can we not make a fire in the stove, if only for an hour, to warm the hut?"

"And how shall the prisoners respect us if we do not share their privations, Comrade? Is it not the policy of our Comrade Political Cadre that we suffer the weather with them, and so dramatize a solidarity that may transcend our distinction in status? We thus take steps to effect their political rehabilitation, do we not? And do we not also meet the challenge presented by a shortage of firewood and coal in this wretched place by this measure of revolutionary discipline? Rouse yourself, Ma, or I shall send you outside!" Ma tries to sit up straight at his small table; he blows into his cupped hands, tucks them under his armpits.

"What I said," says Raleigh Furman Smith, "gabble-talking steady. Don't mean a thing to me, Jim!"

"Raleigh Smith," I say, and pause to choose and arrange my English words before I continue. "I request also you cease reference of address to me as Jim. I am Comrade Interpreter Li. I do not mock you with names of slangs or other vulgarism, can you not reciprocate? Also please no more shit and ass and mother, than which latter I comprehend as diminutive of specific foul obscenity. And also please not to characterize my language as cluckings of fowl! Do I mock your argot? We must communicate, Raleigh Furman Smith!"

"You jive is all you doing, Comrade," he says, and, "What you bring me all the way in here out of my work for, man? What I got to do with damn Boggs fixed out on that wheel with all the garbage and toilet stink?"

"Whilst you progressed here from hence," I say to him, "Comrade Ma undertook for me a service at my order. He did went and gaze upon Lester Boggs suffer his just punishments. Can you guess, Prisoner Smith, as to his report of your comrade's disposition in extreme durance?"

"Lester Boggs?" Smith says, and, "If I know him his butthole be sucking blue pond water! You tell me, Comrade. Saying maybe how he appreciates all of a sudden like the wisdom of Marx and all that dialect hoo-ha if you'll just untie him? Calling out for his mama to come all the way over here to damn Korea and save his Okie behind from that wheel before it gets dark and freezes to him?"

"You are perceptive, Raleigh Smith!" I say, and, in Mandarin to Ma, "Say again to me what you observed of the prisoner in the refuse pit, Ma."

Ma blinks, straightens up to show that he is awake, alert

before he speaks. "Prisoner Boggs wept and shouted many words I could not understand, Comrade Interpreter."

"Yet there was one word you repeated to me. Repeat it again, please, Ma."

"The prisoner cried out *Mama*. Again and again he cried out this word, *Mama*, Comrade. This I heard clearly, and committed it to memory so that I might tell you."

"When you people going to learn I don't speak no Chink, never will!" Raleigh Furman Smith says.

"Chink is pejorative vulgarism!" I say, and, quickly, before he can retort with further insolence, "Did you not hear what Comrade Ma said? *Mama*! *Mama* is the word Lester Boggs says upon the wheel whereto he is affixed in punishments! As you perceived, Raleigh Smith, Comrade Prisoner Boggs calls on his mother for surcease! Are you not affected, Raleigh, that your comrade so suffers as to call upon his mother? Is such revelation not affecting your sensibilities, Raleigh Furman Smith? Do you not feel pang of empathic fellow feeling for your compatriot so distraught?"

"Chink ain't nothing but the same as Chinaman, Comrade. It ain't like saying gook or slope," says Prisoner Raleigh Furman Smith, "and I ain't studying no sorrows for Lester Boggs's troubles. Man," he says, "I wouldn't piss on no part of him if his dumb Okie self was frying in hell instead of freezing to death in your damn garbage dump! Telling me Lester Boggs is hurting? Man, now tell me some *bad* news! And turn me loose back to digging turnips so I can pass it on to all the blood, Jim, give us all a laugh while we steady digging up them turnips!"

"No solidarities with your fellow oppressed, Raleigh Smith?" I say, and, "Do you learn nothing gleaned from discussion of dialectic, Raleigh Smith? How shall you and your Negroid comrades effect liberation if you reject miseries such as Lester Boggs in dire durance? Do you not see, Raleigh

Smith, no man, Negro or not, exists in historical vacuums? Social consciousness, Raleigh Smith," I tell him, "mandates you join ranks, Negroid and Caucasian, strive in communion efforts to throw off shackles forged by historical capitalist bosses who oppress! How else shall you have come to attain to potentials for revolutionary ascendance, Corporal Raleigh Furman Smith?"

He does not answer me, smirks at me, shakes his head, as if to say my words are incoherent, an idiot's prattle. "Do not pretend failure to comprehend, Raleigh Smith! This is familiar ploy to me. What and if I shall proffer to you and Negroid comrades opportunity to effect mitigations of Lester Boggs punishments? Shall you extend hand of cooperativeness, and so make revolutionary nobility of matters now sordid and mundane?"

"Say what?"

I take great care with my speech! "Prisoner Corporal Raleigh Furman Smith," I say, "if you shall have agreed to lead yourself and comrade Negroes in cooperativeness efforts, it is my authority to order Prisoner Boggs released from durance upon wheel in pit. Together, Raleigh Smith, Negroid, Caucasians, valiant soldiers of heroic Chinese Volunteer Army may progress to enlightenment period of dialectic, new eras of social harmony cooperativeness. Shall you not agree, Raleigh Smith?"

"Run that by me one more time, Comrade," he says, and his smile is wide and bright now. "You saying if I get straight with you and the rest of the Chinks here, you going to cut Boggs loose of that wheel before he freezes through?"

"You are perceptive, Prisoner Smith."

"And you the same folks feeds me on turnips make everyone crap like a damn elephant?"

"We share stringent rations, do we not? Also noodles and rice, beans and turnips for roughage bulks. Diet of revolution is not luxury, Raleigh Smith!"

"And you the cat steady threatening me with time in the garbage dump for talking back to them dumb-ass guards?"

"Geneva Convention," I tell him, "cursing forbidden, contrary to good orders and disciplines."

"And, like, for instance, what you want from me, Comrade? What I mean is, lay it out, Jim! Say what it is I gots to do before you going to make it all sweet for us?"

"As follows," I say, and, "Cooperativeness spirit of constructive fervor overall. Sharing of goals and ideals in good faiths, like unto rations we share in this bad place, Raleigh Smith. To wit, specifics: cease cursing of comrade guards in your exotic argot. Enthusiasms of participation in prescribed discussion of dialectic, this only so that revolutionary political education enlightenment may emerge, engendering true exchanges of cultural and political nexus, and most important, ceasing historical antagonisms betwixt Caucasians and Negroids. Latter, I have confidence, shall have resulted if you lead to liberate said Boggs through agreed cooperativeness. I envision revolutionary spirit of understandings mutual, glorious time of union community here in this bad place whilst we throw back revisionist forces of imperialists! Do you comprehend me, Raleigh Smith?"

"Ain't this a bitch?" says Raleigh Furman Smith, and, "Man, you are so dim! What the *hell* I care about damn Lester Boggs! Boggs? Man, I catch his ofay bootie walking my street in Detroit ever, I stick a shank in him fast as spit on him! And your dialect shit you and that political cadre cat Soo steady talking ain't nothing but some bullshit, Jim! Man, turn me loose to go dig them turnips!"

"Comrade," Ma says, stands up at his small table, "does the prisoner grow belligerent? Shall I summon a guard?"

"Sit and be silent!" I command him in Mandarin. To Raleigh Furman Smith, I say, "Rejection? You doubt sincerities perhaps of my heartfelt innermost proposals? Think you I am not honest, Raleigh Smith?"

"Honest?" he says, and, "Man, don't do me no damn favors! Don't you know I ain't no soldier? In real life, man, back in Detroit, I'm the best pimp you ever seen! You honest? You a liar and a ee-lapper, a four-day creeper and a turd-snapper! Jim, if I had you in Detroit, I would cut your stones in a minute!"

Ma says, "Comrade, I will go outside and summon a guard!"

"Sit!" I command him. I say to Raleigh Smith, "You curse me, I think, Prisoner Smith! You iterate ass and say also turd of me, than which is I think synonym of English shit! Shall you wish to join Boggs upon said wheel, Raleigh Smith?"

"I give a rat's ass, Jim," he says, and, "You done called me in here from my work and give out all this gabble, I don't know nothing from what you saying, man!"

"It is my authority to decree punishments, Raleigh Smith!" I say, and, "You transcend camp good order and disciplines! Yet I shall not provoke, yet caution you to consider my words! Think if Lester Boggs succumbs to cold weathers, you also assume responsibility now! You kill your comrade Lester Boggs if you refuse cooperativeness, Prisoner Smith! I do not oppress," I tell him, "only maintain maintenance of orders and disciplines and participate in heroic struggle of People's War!"

"You a liar and a penny-wink," he says. "You eat cat shit and your breath stinks!"

"Summon a guard, Ma!" I command. "This prisoner's attitude is counterrevolutionary! Return him to his work in the fields, and instruct the comrade guard-escorts to listen closely to anything he may say to them, for if he utters even the least vile word I am able to recognize, I will sentence him to join his Caucasian comrade upon the wheel in the refuse pit!"

"You a liar," says Raleigh Furman Smith, "and a pee-weight. Your backbone's crooked and you can't shit straight!"

"You mistake my benevolence!" I shout after him as he is

taken away by Comrade Guard-Escort Hong to return to the turnip fields.

"This is the one," Hong says as he leaves, "who deserves severe punishment! This is the one you always fail to punish for his dirty speech!"

"Are you ill, Comrade Interpreter?" Ma asks when we are alone. "Your hands tremble, Comrade. Your eyelid twitches, and your lips quiver. Do you have a fever, or is it only the cold?"

"Please do not speak, Comrade Ma," I say to him. "I must think, and to think clearly, one must choose words with care, and I cannot bring words to bear upon this problem if you constantly interrupt me."

I say to myself: Li, there is no problem so great that it will not yield to the instrument of dialectical analysis; there is no problem so great that it will not yield to the force of human reason; there is no problem so great that it will not yield to the wondrous order of language!

But it is as if I had no words.

I think: Li, you must search the wisdom of masters Marx and Engels, Comrades Lenin and Stalin, Mao and Chou, the strategies and tactics of People's War as pronounced by Comrade Lin Piao—surely they will show the way!

I think: Li, consider the truths contained in that exquisite tradition of literature you have studied—is there no insight to be discovered in the proletarian fictions of T. Dreiser or J. Farrell, the voices of the masses who sing in the poems of W. Whitman, the dramatized dialectics of H. Fast or M. Gold?

It is as if I know nothing.

There is only Lester Boggs, a rude peasant of Stillwater, Oklahoma—a keeper of grounds at an obscure agricultural college—bound fast with ropes to a discarded caisson wheel in the camp's refuse pit, where he will die if tonight's weather is very cold. I think to myself: Li, were you not such a one, once, as Prisoner Lester Boggs? Ignorant, vulgar, festering with prejudice and hostility? Benighted, a victim of historical oppression, a creature tortured by the press of social brutality and vicious, exploitative economics, twisted into a monstrous shape scarcely distinct from that of a dumb beast, gifted by nature only with the redeeming possibilities of his faculty of speech?

Yet, I, Li, have been raised to dignity, liberated by People's Revolution, made noble by the cultivation of that same faculty—my words!—so that I might lend my strength to our global struggle of People's War, that I might pledge myself to the liberation of such as Lester Boggs of Stillwater, Oklahoma!

And it is I, Li, who has decreed that Lester Boggs shall remain for twenty-four hours upon the caisson wheel in the refuse pit, where he will surely die.

There is only Corporal Raleigh Furman Smith, a cunning and insolent Negro from the city of Detroit, a procurer of whores! I think to myself: Li, were you not, once, such a one as Raleigh Furman Smith? Plagued by your intelligence, bitterly angry at the injustice of a racist, fascist world that refused you the natural dignity your talents should have earned? And, so, contemptuous of those who would hold out the hand of opportunity, enable you to lift yourself up to the potential of your nature? Blinded by the pain of your frustration to the path of deliverance that lay before you?

Yet I, Li, was gathered into the fold of People's Revolution, guided toward the revelations of revolutionary analysis— chosen to matriculate at the People's Institute for Study of Alien Languages, called now to contribute my precious words to the valiant efforts of our heroic Volunteer Army, placed close to the cutting edge of this mighty enterprise of People's War, here in this wretched place—Prisoner Compound Number Nineteen, near the deserted village of Yong Dong Po!

It is I, Li, who must find the means to reprieve Lester Boggs from his sentence of death in the cold, rehabilitate the counterrevolutionary obstructionism of Raleigh Furman Smith, unite them with me in the higher cause that is the only salvation for such as we—Lester Boggs, Raleigh Smith, Li, lover of words.

I dare not despair! And yet, I say to myself: Li, do you think your words, your chaos of lyric Mandarin and muscular English, can do all this?

I do not like Comrade Camp Commandant Duc Fu. He is an old man, too old and frail to take his accustomed place in battle, and I know he hates this, that his age renders him unfit for any duty save this passive garrison life of Prisoner Compound Number Nineteen. I believe he scorns me, young men such as I, Ma, Comrade Political Cadre Soo, the guard-escorts; he is a lifelong soldier, and so believes young men belong in active battle, believes we shirk our duty in this place, has no appreciation of the difficult task we attempt in the revolutionary rehabilitation of the camp's prisoner corps.

Comrade Camp Commandant Duc Fu is an old man, an old soldier, and so I feel the presence of the past when I stand before him in his hut, and I cannot bring myself to like him, for he is of the past, and I do not like to think of the past; People's Revolution is the future, and I prefer the future, which men may, through struggle guided by dialectics, shape to their desired, necessary ends—the past is a chronicle of historical mistakes, however necessary, and though revolution's future builds upon that past, it is still a chronicle of ignorance and oppression, and I cannot like a man who is so wholly of the past.

Yet I must respect Comrade Camp Commandant Duc Fu, not only out of the ethos of revolutionary and military discipline, but also because he has served so long in the great struggle that unites us. He does not often speak of his life, but it is known that he was there on the Long March, served with Mao and Chou in the caves of Hunan, fought bravely and suf-

fered grievous wounds in repelling the fascist Japanese in-
vaders, fought again in the glorious victory over the bloody-
handed Kuomintang. He is too old now, too frail from his
many wounds to fight in battle against Yankee Imperialism and
the running dogs of the puppet Republic of Korea, and I think
fervor and idealism have faded in him. I do not like this man,
but will respect him.

"You have summoned me here, Comrade Camp Commandant," I say.

"Please stand at ease, Comrade Interpreter," says Comrade Duc Fu, and, "While the occasion of my summons is official, I would conduct our interview as informally as possible.
Tell me, Comrade Li, has it grown colder outside during the
last hour? I have not been outside since the calling of roll, and
you see how warm my stove makes my hut. Will you have tea?
Is it colder than when this day began?"

"I cannot say," I tell him. "Perhaps it is not so cold today,
but to stand out in the wind makes it feel very cold. The
weather is always severe in this wretched place," I say. "Terrible cold and snow in winter, hot and dry in summer, and
there is always the wind that blows off the mountains." Comrade Duc Fu smiles.

"People's War requires sacrifice," he says, and, "I think I
feel the cold more than when I was a young man. I could tell
you of the winters we suffered in the caves of Hunan, and on
campaign against the fascist Japanese and the Kuomintang."

"I know your sacrifices were great, Comrade Camp Commandant. They have earned you and your heroic comrades the
undying respect of all true revolutionaries." Comrade Duc Fu
smiles again.

"I take comfort in your generous words, Li," he says,
and, "An old soldier takes such comfort as he can find. Are
you not too warm in your coat, Comrade? You see that the fire
burns nicely in my stove; remove your coat and enjoy the
warmth while we talk."

"I do not feel free to enjoy your fire," I say to him. "I am surprised you make a fire in your stove. Comrade Political Cadre Soo has said that we should set revolutionary examples for the prisoner corps by sharing their necessary privations. Comrade Soo says that if the prisoners see us eat their meager rations and suffer the cold with them, it will gain their confidence, and we may hope to lead them to correct attitudes the more easily, overcoming their hostility." Comrade Camp Commandant Duc Fu closes his eyes, sighs loudly, opens his eyes to look at me.

"Do you presume to instruct me in my duty, Li?" he asks.

"Of course not, Comrade. I only say what I believe." He smiles at me.

"Comrade Soo is an ideologue. That is his duty. I am a soldier. I am also an old man, and so understand things a young man like Soo cannot. He is liable to mistakes due to his inexperience. And you are also a young man, Comrade Li."

"Have I made a mistake, Comrade Camp Commandant? Is this why you summon me to your hut?" Comrade Duc Fu smiles and shakes his head.

"There has been a complaint," he says.

"Lodged by Guard-Escort Hong?" I say. Comrade Duc Fu nods, still smiling; I know that he means me to understand that he is not angry, that he likes me, and yet, though I must and will respect him, I cannot like this man—it is wrong of him to make a fire in his hut's stove when Comrade Soo has said we must share the prisoners' discomfort if we are to rehabilitate them. "He complains of the punishment I decreed for Prisoner Lester Boggs? I assure you, Comrade Duc Fu, the severity of the punishment was merited! Lester Boggs has repeatedly violated the rule of camp good order and discipline that forbids cursing the guards who supervise his work in the turnip fields. I have a ledgerbook, Comrade, which records in precise detail . . ."

Comrade Duc Fu raises his hand to interrupt me, still smiling. "Comrade Hong does not complain of the punishment you mete out to this Lester Boggs. Nor do I question your authority in this matter, Comrade Interpreter. Comrade Hong complains to me that you abused him by humiliating him in the presence of this prisoner named Boggs, and, further, that you exceeded your authority by summoning yet another prisoner, one Smith, a Negro, to your hut when there had been no report to you of his having uttered vile language."

"Comrade Hong was insolent," I say, and, "If I humiliated him, it was to enforce revolutionary and military discipline."

"Perhaps," says Comrade Duc Fu. "And what of this Smith you ordered brought to your hut?"

"Prisoner Lester Boggs accused me of ignoring the violations of the Negro prisoners, Comrade." I say. "I summoned Raleigh Furman Smith to my hut to demonstrate to all that I exhibit no favoritism. Raleigh Smith is, I am certain, also repeatedly guilty of cursing his guard-escorts, but I am unable to establish this due to the exotic argot spoken by him and his Negro comrades. I also seek to use the occasion of Lester Boggs's punishment to effect a solution to the racist factionalism that divides the prisoner corps. I seek to advance toward the goal of prisoner rehabilitation pronounced for us by Comrade Political Cadre Soo. I do not think I have exceeded my authority, Comrade Camp Commandant. I have only sought to bring my skill as an interpreter of English to bear upon the ongoing struggles of People's War and People's Revolution." Comrade Duc Fu covers his mouth with his hand to conceal his smile. I am uncomfortable in the heat of this hut, begin to perspire in my padded coat.

"And how, Comrade Li, shall punishing this prisoner Boggs with death by freezing this night in the refuse pit effect such a miraculous rehabilitation of the prisoner corps?" Comrade Duc Fu mocks me—it is easy for the old to mock the young. For one who heats his hut to mock one who suffers cold for a higher purpose. For an old man who has known only the soldier's life to mock one who seeks a subtler solution to a problem of dialectics—and yet, I will respect Comrade Duc Fu!

"I have offered to release Prisoner Lester Boggs from the

wheel in the refuse pit if Raleigh Furman Smith will pledge to lead his Negro comrades in cooperation, to cease cursing the comrade guard-escorts in their argot, to show enthusiasm for the discussions of dialectics led by Comrade Soo, to cease their counterrevolutionary hostility to the Caucasian prisoners such as Lester Boggs."

"And does this Smith accept your offer, Comrade?"

"Not as yet, Comrade, but I am not discouraged. Dialectics teaches us that despair is not permitted." Comrade Duc Fu is silent for a moment; he closes his eyes, folds his hands before him on the surface of his desk, bows his head, as if deep in thought. I stand at ease before him, listen to the pop and crackle of the fire in his stove, perspire in my padded coat.

"Li," he says, lifts his head, opens his eyes, "does your dialectics tell you what shall become of the prisoner Lester Boggs if his Negro comrade persists in his defiance? What of Lester Boggs, Comrade Li, when night falls in this place?"

"I will hope to effect my solution well before the hour when night falls, Comrade."

"But if you fail? Tell me, Li, what then of Lester Boggs? Can you not speak the words to me, Li?"

I stand at attention before I speak. "He may die, Comrade Camp Commandant. Unless," I add quickly, "there should be some change in the weather. It is always possible that the wind may shift, that it will not be so cold tonight as to cause his death by freezing. I hope to succeed, Comrade."

Comrade Duc Fu smiles again, shakes his head. "Li," he says, "you are a very young man. Let me speak to you as an old man of much experience. Will you listen to my words, Comrade Li?"

"It is my duty to be instructed by you, Comrade Camp Commandant."

"Then attend my words, Li. As we talk here in the warm comfort of my hut, a man lies tied to a caisson wheel in the refuse pit. The wind drives the cold into his bones even as I speak to you. As the day wanes, it can only grow colder. It may even snow this night! A man named Lester Boggs dies as we talk, Li! And why does he die?"

"If he dies," I say, "it is only an incidental death. His death results from a punishment prescribed for his repeated violations of the camp's good order and discipline, which is in turn prescribed by the Geneva Convention. It is not I who cause his death, Comrade! And he dies because the Negro prisoner Raleigh Smith stubbornly persists in his counter-revolutionary defiance of me, because Raleigh Furman Smith will not seize the opportunity I present to him."

"There is no need to shout, Li," says Comrade Duc Fu. "I am an old man; the wounds I have suffered in many battles have left me infirm, but I am not deaf."

"Forgive me, Comrade."

"It is forgiven. Listen to me, Li. You speak words, and you speak loudly with the emotion that animates your belly, but what you say is only words. Is it not the truth of this matter that this Boggs dies because he uttered vile words in his language? Is it not that the Negro Smith will not pronounce some words you wish to hear? Do we not have sufficient slaughter in battle? Do not thousands of our comrades of the Volunteer Army perish at the hands of our enemies? Do not more thousands of our enemies and their running-dog henchmen fall to the guns of our comrades? How many die of this winter's cold, Li, as they lie in their trenches, or lie wounded in the valleys and on the sides of mountains in this desolate country we struggle to liberate? What of the oppressed masses we fight to liberate, Li, have not thousands upon thousands of them died?"

I am only able to say, "I seek to lend my strength toward the inevitable triumph of People's War, Comrade!"

"Li," Comrade Duc Fu says, shakes his head, sighs, "Li, you are not a soldier. You are a student of language, is this not so?"

"I matriculated at the People's Institute for Study of Alien Languages in Hangkow until I was called to join my comrades of our heroic Volunteer Army," I am able to say.

"Li," he repeats, "you are a student of language, not a soldier. You are sent here only because we must have someone who speaks the language of the prisoners placed in our custody. We are far from the battles, Li! Must you kill this man Boggs, for some words, to serve the People's War? Do you care so much for your words that you will kill a man, Li? Can you tell me that some words in his English are of such value that you would kill him for them?"

My body is drenched with perspiration under my padded coat. I feel dizzy, must close my eyes, swallow hard, breathe deeply before I can speak. "I perform my duty," I say, and, "The words of English are mine as well as Boggs's," and, "A word is only a sign of a thing, but if we are indifferent to the meanings of words, then we are indifferent to things, and we thus fail to conduct our lives in concert with the precepts of revolutionary dialectics, and our lives become meaningless. This is the significance of words, without which there is no order and no meaning, no purpose . . ." I cannot speak further; I breathe deeply of the thick warm air of Comrade Duc Fu's hut, afraid I will faint.

"You are distressed, Comrade Li," he says, and, "I am only an old soldier, unqualified to dispute such matters with a student of language. I only know how to kill men in battle, and how to die there if I must. Even now, as you know, Li, the leadership of our Volunteer Army and those who lead our gallant allies in this war meet with the Yankees and their running dogs at Panmunjon to arrange the end of this war. If it does not end soon, still, it will end, and we will return these prisoners to their comrades, and we will welcome the return of thousands of our comrades now held as prisoners. When this comes to pass, Li, shall we have to say that we cannot return Lester Boggs to his comrades because he dies here tonight in this place, killed by some vile words you say he spoke? Can you not answer me, Li?"

I am able to say, "I know only what I know, Comrade."

And then we do not speak for a time; I feel the wetness of my perspiration on my skin, hear the crackle of the fire in the stove, breathe the heavy, warm air of the hut.

Then Comrade Duc Fu says to me, "Do as you must, Comrade Interpreter Li. But do also two things which I shall ask of you. Will you do this?"

"I accept your instruction, Comrade Camp Commandant!"

"Then do these two things: go and discuss this with Comrade Political Cadre Soo—perhaps his dialectics will illuminate your thinking—and go, first, now, Comrade Li, to the refuse pit and look upon this man Boggs. Speak to him. Observe how he fares at this moment, and think how he may fare when night falls. Will you do as I ask?"

"I will, Comrade."

"Then go, now, Li," says Comrade Duc Fu, and I leave his hut. I walk to the far end of the camp compound, to the latrine trenches and the refuse pit. I cringe in my padded coat against the wind-driven cold that burns on my streaming skin, flecks of blowing snow in the air stinging my wet face.

I say to myself: Li, a man can survive in this cold; it is not so cold that a man will, of necessity, die!

I only feel the cold so because I have just come from the warmth of Comrade Duc Fu's hut stove, and because my skin is wet with perspiration, and because I walk across the prison compound, where the wind rushes freely down from the distant mountains—in the camp's refuse pit, bound to the caisson wheel, there will be shelter from the wind. There, it is almost as if a man were in his hut, cold, but not so cold that he will, of necessity, freeze to death.

I say to myself: men survive cold. I think of the fictions of J. London, of the story of the man who walked across frozen wastes much colder than this wretched place, so cold the man's spittle froze solid before it hit the hard crust of snow he walked upon, and his breath frosted his beard, and large trees split open with a sound like gunfire in the cold.

I remember the story, that the man would have survived had he not stepped through thin ice over a stream, wet his feet—and still he would have survived, had he been able to build a fire to dry and warm his feet . . .

"Boggs," I say, and, "Comrade Prisoner Boggs, it is I, Comrade Interpreter Li. Open eyes and look at me, Boggs. I come to speak to you. How fare you, Boggs?"

"You damn sumbitch!" Boggs says, but he does not open his eyes, does not look at me.

The wind does not blow so hard down here in the refuse pit; the pit itself, and the heaped mounds of camp garbage do give shelter from the hard wind, the tiny snowflakes only drift down in the air, lightly dust the garbage mounds white, dust white the caisson wheel that is propped against a solid pile of camp garbage, dust white the form of Prisoner Lester Boggs, tied by both arms to the wheel, his legs stretched out on the littered ground that is dusted white by the tiny snowflakes that drift down out of the wind, into the refuse pit.

"Lester," I say, "it is I, Li. I inquire of your welfare. Will you not speak to me, Lester Boggs?" The stench of the nearby latrine trenches lies like a foul blanket over the refuse pit, pierces the antiseptic cold to clog my nostrils, clutch at my throat. "It is not so bad, I think, Lester," I say, "save that stink of excrement pervades, is it not so?" Lester Boggs opens his eyes.

"Why you killing me, man?" he says.

"Prescribed punishments, Lester," I say, and, "Geneva Convention," and, "Camp good orders and disciplines," and, "Are you in hurt, Lester?"

"You mean-assed bastard!" he says, and, "I never even said what fucking Hong said I said!"

"Prevarication, Lester!" I say. "Too late for mitigations now. Yet I shall convey no personal intent! Do you comprehend me? Further, possibilities of remittance abound! Do you hear me? Prisoner Corporal Raleigh Furman Smith may yet agree to cooperations, upon which I vow to release you from decreed durance, Lester! Do you comprehend? Words uttered may be renounced, upon which I return you to ranks of your comrades before eventide. Thereafter, dawning era of cooperations amongst all concerned, do you comprehend?"

I do not think Lester Boggs listens to me, does not understand. He says nothing, only sags upon the caisson wheel. I listen to the wind shriek above the mounds of camp garbage, hold my breath to stop the stench of the latrines. Lester Boggs begins to whimper; he draws his feet up, turns his head from side to side, like a petulant child who resists sleep. He coughs and spits before he can speak.

"They took me out of Stillwater, Oklahoma, where I had me my first good job up to the A & M college," he says, "and made me go soldier at Fort Leonard Wood, made me live right in the same barracks with niggers and all kinds of trash, and then they sent me here and I got took prisoner; it wasn't none of it my fault, and now they're killing my ass when I never done nothing to nobody!"

"Lester," I say, "I am reported you cry out for succor to mother. Not a man's thing to do, Lester! Please demonstrate courage! Think you not I also have mother and father and siblings far away in Hangkow city? Oftentimes of eventide, alone in hut save for the ignorant peasant Ma, I do think upon family and wish once again to be as before, matriculant of People's Institute for Study of Alien Languages, Lester, but do not request succor of my mother or father or remote siblings. I act the man, Lester! I too experience despair, though same is forbidden by dialectic, and so strive to pervert my mind to lesson of dialectic, practice skills of language via perusal of glossaries by light of candle so that I shall speak more facile your English, Lester! Do you comprehend me?"

"Man!" Lester Boggs cries out; his voice seems to echo among the mounds of garbage, to echo back to us from the wind.

"Man," says Lester Boggs, "I'm freezing my ass to death, Comrade! I can't hardly feel nothing in my hands, they tied the rope too tight! I can't feel my toes on my feet, man! My feet feels like that they turned to wood inside my boots, man! I'm hurting, Comrade! My face is all numb feeling, can't you help me, man?"

I am very careful as I choose the words to speak to him. "Lester Boggs," I say, "I seek your salvations. I shall persist to prevail against Raleigh Furman Smith's counterrevolutionary revisionism! I venture now to address Comrade Soo for guidance, Lester. Be stout heart, Lester! I, Comrade Li, quest to formulate triumphant solutions of cooperations beneficiality to all!"

"Fucking gook cocksucker!" he shouts after me as I climb back up the steep side of the refuse pit, ascend into the wind that seems stronger now at midday, carrying away the odor of the latrines. I hear the cry of Lester Boggs, faint in the stiffening wind: "Mama!" he cries out to the wind and cold and the awful stench of excrement.

"As you see, Comrade Interpreter," Comrade Political Cadre Soo says, "I am busy, for there is no end to the tasks of People's Revolution and People's War, yet I am always prepared to lend my counsel in matters of significance. Does not the wisdom of our dialectics posit that the attention of a true revolutionary consciousness must remain ever sensitive to each detail within our scrutiny? Speak, Comrade Li, for I listen."

Comrade Political Cadre Soo is at work in his hut, as always, diligently preparing for the discussions of dialectics he conducts for us all, the prisoner corps as well as his comrades of the camp's staff. Seated on the packed-earth floor, he wields an ink brush, letters squares of rice paper with the calligraphy of revolutionary aphorisms: *The Revolution Is Greater Than The Self*; *Serve The Revolution!*; *All Labor Dignifies The Revolution!*; *Correct Attitudes Foster Revolutionary Ardor*; *Worker, Peasant, Soldier: People's War Unites Us!*

"I am ordered by the comrade camp commandant to seek your advice in a matter pertaining to the maintenance of the camp's good order and discipline," I say.

"The matter of Prisoner Lester Boggs?" says Comrade Soo.

"Someone has reported this to you, Comrade Political Cadre?"

"Just as it is your duty to interpret the English words spoken by the comrade prisoners, Li, it is mine to know all that can be known of what transpires in the camp, is it not? For, as dialectics teaches us, Comrade, all activity, despite how trivial, is a part of the historical design of People's Revolution, and it is my duty to provide the correct political analysis for all in the affairs of this camp, to lead in the development of revolutionary insight among the ranks of our heroic Volunteer Army, and to serve as a catalyst for the development of revolutionary rehabilitation among the Yankee prisoners entrusted to our custody, is this not so, Comrade Interpreter Li?"

When Comrade Soo speaks of revolution, of dialectics, there is an animation in his voice, an expression of true zeal in his eyes that makes me forget the cold that grips my flesh; his words obliterate the whistling wind that buffets the thin walls of his hut—the integrity of his vision, the firm conviction of his belief, are like an armor he never ceases to wear, protecting him against the elements of weather, the specters of doubt and confusion that assail me in this wretched place. I have only the words of English that I love, my Mandarin, the fragile beauty of literature.

I can only wish sometimes that I were such a man as Comrade Soo, or even Comrade Duc Fu—the duties of ideologists and soldiers are always clear; the meanings of words, even in my graceful Mandarin, seem sometimes to me so shifting and insubstantial, like powdery snow driven into the fluid shapes of drifts by a winter wind.

"I do not think the matter is trivial, Comrade."

"I quite agree, Comrade," he says. "It is not a trivial matter. But you perhaps do not discern the true nature of its import."

"There is the possibility that a man may die of the punishment I decreed, Comrade," I say to him.

"You are mistaken, Comrade Interpreter," he says, and, before I can speak, "It is true that Prisoner Boggs may well perish of the cold in the refuse pit this night. Rather, it is a certainty he will freeze to death, Comrade. But this is as nothing against the threat that exists to the revolutionary solidarity of our ranks! It is regrettable if a prisoner should die, Comrade Li, but it might prove fatal to the cause of People's War if you are set against—or set yourself against—the comrade guard-escorts."

"Comrade Hong has spoken with you!" I say.

"It was his duty to do so," says Comrade Soo, "and I commended him for reporting this incident to me. It is precisely matters such as this that I am pledged to confront and resolve!"

"Comrade Hong was insolent," I say, and, "He attempts to interfere with my authority," and, "I have already begun to take measures that will resolve the problem!"

"Softly, Li!" says Comrade Soo. "Correct analysis requires a head clear and free of the belly's subjective emotions. Will you listen and be guided by me?" he asks.

"That is my duty."

"Listen, then, Comrade Li. Comrade Hong accuses you of favoritism on behalf of the Negro prisoners—"

"This is a lie!" I interrupt, but Comrade Soo does not stop to hear me.

"—the truth of which complaint is of no consequence. Be silent, please! What is true is that Comrade Hong and his comrades perceive it to be true. Our first imperative is to maintain solidarity with our own comrades. Thereafter, we may address the rehabilitation of the prisoner corps. Thus, it is clear that you must heal this breach between yourself and Comrade Hong."

"Comrade," I say quickly, "I have already begun to do so!"

"In what fashion, Comrade Interpreter?"

"I have spoken with the prisoner Raleigh Furman Smith, who is esteemed by his Negro comrades as a leader, and whose model they emulate."

"Prisoner Smith is known to me, Comrade," says Comrade Soo, and, "He is a counterrevolutionary influence in this camp, ridden with the disease of fascist racist factionalism, as revisionist as this Boggs who expires in the refuse pit even as we talk here in my hut! Have we not both noted how he resists the discussions of dialectics? Is he not a sullen, obstructionist personality? Is he not the very man Comrade Hong complains you favor by failing to punish his filthy speech?"

"I do not spare him out of favoritism, Comrade Soo," I say, and "Raleigh Furman Smith and his Negro comrades escape punishment so often only because my English is not adequate to the precise translation of the argot they speak. Though I was called away from my course of study at the People's Institute for Study of Alien Languages, I continue to peruse my English glossaries, and to read in the tradition of their literature in the hopes that my skills will improve, that I will be able to understand their obscure obscenities, and thus render punishments just to all, I . . ."

"Bourgeois prattle, Comrade Interpreter!" Comrade Soo says, and he rises from the floor, steps away from his brush and ink pot and the squares of rice paper lettered with the calligraphy of revolutionary aphorisms; he faces me to deliver his lecture.

"Li," he says, "you are a young man of much promise. And you occupy a position of serious responsibility here. You may perhaps think of yourself only as a student of language . . ."

"I pledge my skills to the struggle of People's War," I say, but he does not hear me, continues to speak.

" . . . and though Comrade Hong may think you arrogant

and unfit to be entrusted with the discipline of the comrade prisoners, and Camp Commandant Duc Fu respects only soldiers, whose struggle takes place in the heat of battle, I, Soo, Political Cadre Officer of Prisoner Compound Number Nineteen, say to you that your role as camp interpreter is of equal importance to the function of the comrade guard-escorts, or Comrade Duc Fu's, or even to the role of our valiant soldiers of the heroic Volunteer Army who face the enemy on the battlefield!"

"I try to believe this!" I say.

"You must believe it, Comrade Li! Is not one of the lessons of dialectics that the role of each comrade, no matter how humble or remote from the leading edge of the revolution, is vital to the success of revolution?"

"I understand this," I say.

"Then hear me, and be instructed, Comrade Li! You must go to Comrade Guard-Escort Hong. You must offer him your sincere apology. And then you must demonstrate for him and his comrades that you mean no favoritism on behalf of the Negro prisoners! Do you understand my directive, Comrade?"

"I think I do, Comrade. But I have said I do not exhibit favoritism—it is only the problem of their words! And I have offered Prisoner Raleigh Furman Smith the opportunity of mitigating the punishment of Boggs if he will but vow to cease his obstructionism, if he will but adopt an attitude conducive to rehabilitation through the guidance of the dialectics you teach us . . ."

"Words, Li!" says Comrade Soo, and, "Will you be instructed by the authority of your political cadre officer?" and, "You have attempted to solve your problem with your words, Comrade, but to no avail. It is time for resolute revolutionary action, Comrade! We have all tried to effect prisoner rehabilitation by establishing solidarity with the prisoner corps. Do we not share the privation of their rations, sacrifice our comfort to share even the misery of this weather with them?"

I say, "Comrade Duc Fu burns a fire in his hut stove."

"Comrade Duc Fu is an old man," says Comrade Soo, and, "Perhaps his old bones feel the cold more intensely than ours. Perhaps his revolutionary ardor is weakened by the wounds he suffered in battle, or perhaps his vitality was sapped by the privations of the Long March—it is of no consequence to us, Li! We are young men, and we do not flinch in the throes of the struggle! Nor shall we falter when circumstances dictate a new tactic. Has not Comrade Lin Piao written that victory in People's War falls to the man who adapts his strategy to the moment at hand? It is time, Comrade Interpreter, to go beyond words and provide an example of steadfast revolutionary discipline for all our comrades!"

"Then Lester Boggs shall die this night?" I ask.

"What is the death of one rude Yankee peasant against the success of People's War and People's Revolution, Comrade?"

"And what of Raleigh Furman Smith?" I ask.

"The tree that will not bend must of necessity break—is this not the lesson of dialectics, Comrade?"

"I understand you, Comrade Political Cadre," I say, "but I am uncertain as to how exactly I shall do all you instruct me to perform."

When Comrade Soo smiles, it is as if there is no cold, no wind or snow, as if this wretched place did not exist. When Comrade Soo smiles, places his hand on the shoulder of my padded coat in a gesture of solidarity, it is as if there is only the warming light of revolutionary dialectics, and we bask together in its glow, warmed, lit ourselves by the unshakeable resolution of our faith, the immovable strength of our convictions!

"I am content to leave such particulars to you, Comrade Li," he says, and "You are a man of words, you will find the way to effect what is necessary to the success of the greater purpose we both serve!"

As I leave his hut, Comrade Soo says to me, "Shut the door tightly, Li! With each passing minute, it grows colder outside! The cold threatens to paralyze my fingers, and I have much work yet to do with my brush and ink!" And he blows on his hands to warm them.

I think upon my function here in Prisoner Compound Number Nineteen, here in this wretched place, near the deserted village of Yong Dong Po.

I think of the many classes of instruction I have given for the assembled guard-escorts, how I stood before them, as if I were one of my own revered teachers at the People's Institute for Study of Alien Languages, in Hangkow.

I stand before the assembled guard-escorts in the same large hut where Comrade Soo conducts his discussions of dialectics. As I speak, I look directly into their faces, watch to see that they listen closely, pay strict attention to my words. I make my face a mask of sober, serious concentration, so that they may know how important my words are.

"Listen!" I say to them, and, "Comrades, watch the movement of my lips. Hear what I say in silence, but let your lips move as mine do so that the words I would teach you become your words, so that when you hear these words from the comrade prisoners, it will be as if you yourselves have spoken them. You will recognize them, and know the counterrevolutionary insubordination they express. Quiet, please, Comrades! Do not shuffle your feet, try not to cough, forget the sound the wind makes outside. Listen!"

I lock their eyes with mine, pause a moment before I begin.

"The word we learn today," I say to them, "is *fuck. Fuck,*" I repeat. "This is perhaps the word you shall hear most frequently from the comrade prisoners. *Fuck,*" I say to them, and, "Now, all in concert, repeat after me: *Fuck!* Let me hear you say it together, Comrades, *fuck!*"

Mumbling, slurring, inaccurate, their lips stiff and awkward, heads nodding, shoulders hunched—as if their bodies' motions could force their mouths to open and close with less strain, the assembled guard-escorts say it: *Fuck.*

"Again, Comrades."

"*Fuck.*"

"Yet again."

"*Fuck!*"

"Say it without reserve! Say it with no thought for its possible meaning! Say it with such energy that you may feel the shape of its sound on your tongues. Feel your teeth on your lip, the catch in the back of your throat! Say it again, Comrades, after me, *fuck!*"

"*Fuck!*" the assembled guard-escorts say, their voices joined harmoniously now; some shake their heads, as if they doubt the reality of this alien noise they utter, some smile with satisfaction, some squint at me—as if the new word they speak evidences a wisdom they have always suspected in themselves.

"*Fuck!*" I say to them, and, "Excellent, Comrades! But do not congratulate yourselves prematurely, for the phenomenon of language is less simple than it may first appear. For example, you will not always hear this word from the comrade prisoners thus, in isolation, where its sound can be recognized by the dullest ear. You will as often hear it in the context of other words of their English, words that will sound as alien to you as the honking of geese or the clucking of hens. And this single word exists in variant forms."

"I do not understand what you say, Comrade Interpreter," says one man, his face twisted in a frown of bewilderment. The comrade guard-escorts, I must remind myself, are drawn from the ranks of the most backward, uncultured peasants; illiterate as rocks or trees, they are too ignorant to serve the Volunteer Army except as wardens of the prisoner corps—better, more intelligent men serve in battle against the Yankee Imperialists and their running dogs, even as we gather in the large hut for instruction.

"I mean, Comrades," I tell them, "that the comrade prisoners will not say only this word *fuck* to you. They will say it in combinations of other words, some of them equally vile, and they will speak variations of this word, which will make it more difficult for you to recognize it. For example, Comrades, they may say *fuck you*, or *fucker*, or *fuck off*, or *fuck face*, or *fucking*, *fucked*, and *fuck yourself*, and *fuck you in the ass*, and *fuck around*, or *fuck it*, and there is also the peculiar variant popular with our Negro prisoners, *motherfuck*, which they may also utter in truncated fashion, as *mother*, the unspoken *fuck* being understood as intended by the speaker. There remain even more variants. Even I, who make the study of their English words the work of my life, the weapon I wield in the struggle of this People's War, even I do not know, cannot recognize many exotic and idiosyncratic variations of this basic vile word!"

The assembled guard-escorts are stunned to silence by the possibilities of the word I would teach them, and I fear I have said too much, destroyed their confidence in their ability to learn. Quickly, I say, smiling, "If you but know this root word, recognize it when you hear it, you shall most probably recognize it as the core of most obscene combinations of words the comrade prisoners may utter. And when you hear it, Comrades, what is your duty?"

This question they are able to answer, their voices joined to make one loud collective voice. "Upon hearing vile language uttered, certain that the language is directed at oneself or one's comrade guard-escort, one rehearses the sound of the utterance in order to repeat it distinctly to the comrade camp interpreter at the time this serious infraction of the camp's good order and discipline is reported! Punishment for the infraction will be decreed by the comrade interpreter, and executed at once! In this manner, the camp's good order and discipline will be maintained. In this manner also the authority of the camp guard-escorts will be secured, and the task of the revolutionary rehabilitation of the prisoner corps can proceed, and, thereby, the triumph of both People's War and People's Revolution will be achieved!"

"Excellent, Comrades!" I say, and they smile, laugh, as I, when a student at the People's Institute for Study of Alien Languages, smiled and laughed when praised by my teachers.

"May I ask a question, Comrade Interpreter?" says a man, prodded by a whispering comrade seated beside him.

"Of course."

"What does this English word, *fuck*, signify, Comrade?"

I wait for the giggling to cease before I answer him. When I speak, I make a stern mask of my face so that they shall know I permit no idle levity to disrupt our study.

I say to them, "Comrades, we are not concerned with the nasty meanings of these words I teach you! Our interest is not prurient, nor is it scholarly. It is my role to teach you to recognize vile English words by their sounds; your role is to learn to recognize them when they are uttered by the comrade prisoners, so that you may make your reports to me, so that I may in turn decree punishments that are just. Comrades," I tell them, "learn what I teach you! Leave the meanings of words to me, as it is left to me to decree punishments appropriate to their utterance!"

"Welcome to my hut, Comrade Guard-Escort Hong," I say. When I speak to him, I try to smile to conceal the shame and bitterness I feel for what I must do. "I am grateful," I say, "for your willingness to leave your duty with the comrade prisoners in the turnip fields and come here to talk with me."

"Comrade Ma stated to me that the matter was most urgent, Comrade Interpreter," he says. I search his face with my eyes, but he does not betray that he knows my purpose, does not appear to gloat over his triumph.

"It is most urgent, Comrade," I say, and, "The solidarity of revolutionary comrades, and the solidarity of those who fight side by side for the victory of People's War are matters of the greatest urgency, are they not, Comrade Hong?" When he says nothing, I continue. "Comrade Hong, I offer you my apology if I offended you this morning in the presence of both Comrade Ma and Prisoner Lester Boggs." Now he smiles at me, gloats, reveals his impudence and insolence! "I was persuaded of my error by Comrade Political Cadre Soo, and, thus, I apologize to you so that there shall be no hindrance to our mutual and cooperative efforts to further the glorious cause we serve together."

This impudent, insolent Hong—this dirty, ignorant son of dirty, ignorant peasants!—says nothing! I must say to him, "Will you accept my sincere apology, Comrade?" before he will respond.

"Thank you for your apology, Comrade Li," he says, "which I accept. I would say only that your sincerity would be doubly gratifying if you had allowed Comrade Ma to remain here in the hut with us to witness your words."

I do not allow my face to express what I feel! I shall do what I must, bear such impudent insolence as I must at the hands of this filthy, uncultured peasant! I look without expression into his eyes, swallow, moisten my lips before I can speak.

"I agree," I tell him, "but you must know my purpose in sending him away when he returned with you from the turnip fields, Comrade. If my sincere apology is accepted . . ." I begin.

"It is accepted, Comrade Interpreter," he says.

". . . then I would speak to you of another matter, one I wish Ma to remain ignorant of, one pertaining to the duties we perform here in service to the cause of People's War. I request your cooperation in a matter pertaining to one of the comrade prisoners, Hong."

"In the revolutionary spirit of solidarity," says this damnable Hong, "I extend my full cooperation in any matter of duty, Comrade Li!" Oh, he smiles broadly at me now! "Which of the comrade prisoners do you refer to, Comrade?" he says.

"Prisoner Corporal Raleigh Furman Smith, the Negro." Now his smile is all but a disgusting laugh! And he grins at me, waits for me to continue! "Comrade Prisoner Smith," I say, "is a destructive and obstructionist counterrevolutionary influence in this camp, with regard to his Negro comrades, who follow him in resisting the instruction in dialectics offered for their enlightenment by Comrade Soo, and also with regard to the fascist racist factionalism that impedes the creation of revolutionary solidarity between the Caucasian prisoners and the Negroes." My lips are dry, my tongue hot and sore, my throat parched when I finish uttering these words!

"That is as I have always said to you, Comrade," he says, and, "What shall you require of me?" I fear I will be unable to speak the words, but I am able to speak, and my voice is clear and loud in the chill of my hut, as if the matter were of no more than routine significance.

"I would chastise Prisoner Raleigh Furman Smith. For this, I require a pretext to decree his punishment. I ask that you bring him to me here when the prisoner corps is escorted back to the compound from their work in the turnip fields. I ask that you report to me that he has violated the tenets of the Geneva Convention by uttering to you a vile expression in English, contrary to the camp's good order and discipline. I will then punish him for this infraction." When I have said this, I wonder that I was able to do so, that I am not dizzy, that perspiration does not break out in beads on my face despite the chill of my hut, that my tongue is not paralyzed in my mouth. Hong's smile is unbearable!

"Excellent, Comrade Li!" he says, and, "And were you also persuaded to this by Comrade Soo?"

"No," I say, "it is a strategy of my own formulation. It is a drastic measure," I tell him, "designed to further the cause of prisoner rehabilitation, and one in accord with the principles of dialectics that guide us. I am certain Comrade Soo would approve this strategy."

"And what of Camp Commandant Duc Fu?" this damnable Hong asks. "Will he also approve?"

"I am within my authority," I am able to say—I am struck with wonder at all I am able to say!— "and the approval of Comrade Soo renders Comrade Duc Fu's opinion moot in a matter involving revolutionary dialectics. Will you cooperate?" I ask. Oh, the terrible smile on the face of Comrade

Hong! I must be done with this!

"I will, Comrade. Tell me, what shall I report that the prisoner Smith said to me?"

"Anything," I say, and "Report any vile word of English you know. Say that he said *fuck* to you, or something of the Negro argot, *motherfuck*, or the truncated *mother*. It does not matter what word you report he said!"

"I think it does, Comrade. I must report something authentic, convincing, if we are to demonstrate that the Negro comrade prisoners cannot in future expect to curse me and my comrades with impunity, is this not so?"

"It is," I say.

"Then tell me what to report, Comrade Li. Say the word or words, and I shall rehearse all the while until we return the prisoners to the compound, and I promise I shall render the sound of it with great accuracy. What shall I say he said, Comrade?"

I do not think I shall be able to think of any words; I do not think I shall ever again be able to reach out and choose my beloved English words, ever again, and I am struck with wonder at how easily it comes to me!

"Say of Smith," I say, "that he said to you: *Your mama go down so many times she got to go to the barber to get her teeth shaved.* Can you say that, Hong?"

At first, he cannot, for there are too many words, so I must repeat it, and repeat it for him, and he rehearses the words, and soon he can say them so that even Smith or any of his Negro comrades would understand them. "You are a good student, Hong," I say.

"I go now, Comrade Li," he says, "to rejoin my comrade guards and the prisoner corps in the turnip fields, and will return with Smith when we are all returned to call the roll in the compound. And I shall find Comrade Ma and tell him to return to your hut, so that he will be present to witness and record everything in his book."

"I shall be here," I say.

"This will be a good thing we do, Comrade Li," he says as he leaves, and, "It is amusing! Have you been outside recently, Comrade? On my way here from the fields, I passed near the refuse pit. One can hear the bawling of the prisoner Boggs, carried on the wind!"

"I shall be here," I say.

"If you go outside, Comrade," Hong says before closing the hut's door behind him, "do not fail to button your coat snugly and tie the flaps of your hat under your chin, for it grows much colder. A man could easily frostbite his ears in this wind!"

While I wait, there is nothing to do but wait. I sit, huddling in my padded coat against the cold that penetrates the thin walls of my hut—I try not to listen, but I hear the rising wind that assaults the thin walls of my hut, rattles the door in its frame. I think to go to the door, open it, look out to see if there is more snow in the air, but I do not do this, I can only wait.

I hope that Ma will come soon; I might talk with him—of anything, his life as a peasant in a farming commune, my life as a student of language—perhaps I would not hear the wind, feel the cold, wonder if the snow falls faster and thicker. But Ma does not come for a long time, and I can only wait.

I go to the shelf where I keep my books, my glossaries, novels, volumes of poetry, wrapped in heavy cloths to protect them from the air's damp, but I cannot read, cannot study. The English words in their neat rows are only words, the calligraphs of my delicate Mandarin are only calligraphs—as arbitrary as the weather in this wretched place, as empty in their meanings as Comrade Soo's slogans. There is nothing for me to do but wait.

I think: Li, dare you call yourself a true lover of words if you do this thing? For if I love words, love them as signs of things, the means by which we know things—the beauty and pain and heroic struggle of life—then how dare I corrupt them by what I do, how dare I use them to do a thing corrupt? Li, I say to myself, a true lover of words will not dishonor them, for in so doing you dishonor yourself!

I say to myself: Li, are not men only creatures who speak? Is it not the gift and the sacred tradition of language which elevates men above the condition of beasts? If you violate the gift and this tradition, do you not make a beast of yourself, Li?

I think upon the time when I was a student, seated with my young comrades in the classrooms of the People's Institute for Study of Alien Languages in Hangkow. I try to remember myself then, no more than a boy, my eyes fixed upon the page of a book, my ears alert to the voice of the comrade teacher who spoke the words aloud as we read them—I remember myself forming the shapes of words in my mouth, my tongue against my teeth, lips tingling with the feel of words passing over them to become sound and meaning in the air, in my ears, the ears of my comrade students, the comrade teacher . . .

I can only wait in my cold hut, here in this wretched place near the deserted village of Yong Dong Po, wait, huddling against the cold, hear the rip of the wind that comes from the mountains, wonder about the snow. I cannot study my glossaries, cannot read, so wrap my books again in the cloths that protect them from damp and insects, and I wait. I cannot truly remember that boy who loved the words taught to him at the People's Institute for Study of Alien Languages—I have lost him, betrayed his love, and shall never again be what he was!

I say to myself: Li, that which you were given, you have in turn given away—now, because you do this corrupt thing, you only know words of English and Mandarin; you can no longer truly love them, and so it does not matter what they signify. Ah, Li! Who and what have you become?

"Comrade Clerk Ma," I say, "record that Prisoner Corporal Raleigh Furman Smith is brought to me on report by Comrade Guard-Escort Hong, who charges him with a violation of the camp's good order and discipline, in that he alleges the comrade prisoner did curse him in vile words of English." Ma rubs his hands together to warm them, flexes his fingers. He licks the point of his pen, dips it in the inkpot, begins the laborious scrawl of his calligraphy.

"What the damn hell you calling me out from ranks for, man?" says Raleigh Furman Smith, and, "I been digging damn turnips make us crap from eating them in the cold all afternoon. I need to be answering my name at roll call outside, man . . ." We hear bugles blowing, distorted by the wind, calling the prisoner corps to attention for roll call.

"Stand silence, Comrade Prisoner," I say, and, "Speak solely as spoken of, Comrade," and, "We pursue seriousness officially!"

"It is very amusing, Comrade," Hong says, grinning.

"Please do not smile or otherwise express levity, Comrade," I say to him, and, "My clerk records this proceeding in our camp's ledger. Let us act with due decorum, please!" Hong bites his lip to stop smiling. I wait an instant before continuing, choose the English words.

"Comrade Prisoner Smith," I say, "this comrade guardescort reports as how you curse him with languages most filthy!"

"Say what?" Smith says.

"Comrade Hong is reporting of your nasty talk uttered to him of this afternoon whilst in pursuits of respective duties assigned!"

"You a damn lie!" says Raleigh Furman Smith, but I turn away from him to speak to Hong.

"Repeat to me now, please Comrade, the words the comrade prisoner did utter, as exactly as you can recall them!" Hong cannot stop his face from forming a grin as he speaks.

"The prisoner," he says, "said to me: *You mama go down to barber teeth shave!*"

"What the hell . . ." Raleigh Smith says before I can speak to him.

"Accusing you of utterances vile, Prisoner Smith! As following: Your mama go down so many times she got to go to the barber to get teeth shaved! This I recognize as lewd references couched obscene in argot you parlance amongst dark hue peers, not so? How plead to allegations, Prisoner Smith? Answer me, please!"

"He says I says . . ." says Smith, and, "Man, I can't even tell what the hell's he's talking!" and, "Man, you pulling some shit on me, Li?"

"Stand silence!" I command, and, "Inadequate response, Prisoner Smith!" and, "I decree guilty as how alleged, punishments of four and twenty hours durance upon wheel alongside Comrade Boggs!" and, to Ma, the change from English to my Mandarin so effortless is to seem as though they were but one language. "Record the charge and the punishment I decree, Ma! Twenty-four hours upon the wheel! I will devise a calligraph for the obscenity."

"You motherfucker!" screams Raleigh Furman Smith, and, "Motherfucker, I'll have your ass!"

"See how this arrogant devil bellows, Comrade," Hong says.

"You compound offenses with vileness, Raleigh Smith!" I say, and then Raleigh Furman Smith leaps upon me, clutches my throat with his fingers, and we fall to the earthen floor; I try to speak, but his fingers pinch my throat, and he rages at me, his mouth touching my ear.

"You doing me this shit 'cause I won't save that cracker's white bootie, motherfucker!" he says. "I'll kill your motherfucking gook ass!" I try to speak, but cannot, hear Ma cry out for help, that the comrade prisoner is killing me, and then Hong strikes Raleigh Furman Smith with the butt of his rifle, and his fingers release my throat, and he rolls off me, moans, "Kill your gook ass," and Ma helps me to stand.

"Shall I hit him again, Comrade?" Hong says, raises his rifle to strike.

"Are you injured, Comrade Interpreter?" Ma says, and, "I think the prisoner would have killed you!"

"There is no need to hit him again, Hong," I say, and, "Take this comrade prisoner to the refuse pit, bind him to the wheel alongside Lester Boggs, as I have decreed."

"Man," Prisoner Raleigh Furman Smith moans, "man, you broke my fucking head, man! My head's busted, I can't see shit, motherfuckers!" he moans, holds his bleeding head with both hands, rolls from side to side in pain on the packed-dirt floor of my hut.

"He assaulted you, Comrade Li," Hong says. "We must report this to the Comrade Camp Commandant. We shall have him beaten for this! He should be executed for this!"

"Are you not hurt, Comrade Interpreter?" Ma is saying.

"There is no need," I tell Hong. "He will die there in the refuse pit with Lester Boggs. Help the prisoner to his feet, Comrade Hong. Escort him now to the refuse pit. Do as I ask, please. We have done what we said we would do."

"Stand up, Yankee devil!" Hong shouts, jerks Raleigh Furman Smith to his feet. Raleigh Smith cannot stand straight, holds his bleeding head with both hands. "I shall take him to the refuse pit, Comrade," Hong says. "I shall escort him past the ranks of the prisoners gathered for roll call, and they will see his bloody face and hear him cry with pain, and there will be no more cursing of me and my comrades by the Yankee prisoners, not the dark devils or the light shall dare curse us in their stupid language when they know both he and Boggs freeze together on the wheel—oh, it is amusing, Comrade!"

"Go, please, Comrade. Ma," I say, "write in the ledger as I instructed."

"Shall I write that the prisoner assaulted you, Comrade Li?"

"Write," I tell him, "only what I have said to write!"

"You a damn lie, Li!" Raleigh Furman Smith is able to say when he reaches the hut's door, dragged by Hong. "You putting your lying shit on my ass, man."

"You refuse cooperations efforts," I say to him, and, "What now of Lester Boggs? You suffer suffering in solidarities now, Raleigh Smith!" and, "What of words spoken nor not when lofty idealisms goals effected, Raleigh Furman Smith?" and, "Dialectic dictates strategies in service of People's Revolution and People's War, Raleigh Furman Smith!"

"Do not waste your words on this arrogant Yankee devil, Comrade," Hong says as he pulls Smith out the door, and, "He will speak more gently to those in authority if by a miracle he survives this night!"

"Lie, man!" Smith shouts, unsteady, stumbling, holding his head, blood on his hands and face and the sleeves of his coat. "You all a damn lie and that's all it is, motherfucking gook motherfuckers!"

"Stick and stone, Raleigh Smith!" I shout after him, and, "Words avail naught versus historic necessaries!"

"Comrade," Ma says when they have gone, "are you well? I do not think you appear well. Shall I prepare tea for you to drink? Shall I make a fire in the stove to restore you?"

"I am well, Ma," I say to him. "Write what I have told you in the ledger. We are done with this."

From outside, I hear the icy sound of the bugles as they make the final announcement of roll call. I go to the door of my hut, open it, look out to see the prisoner corps assembled in ranks in the compound. I hear the faint growl of their voices as they observe Raleigh Furman Smith dragged, bleeding, away to the refuse pit.

I let the cold embrace me, feel the driven snowflakes strike my face, see the thin white coat of snow that covers the compound now, paints white the ranks of the prisoner corps assembled for roll call. The sky seems lower, closer now, and it is already darker, night falling fast in this wretched place.

"When you devise the new calligraphs for me, I will finish writing the entry in the book," May says, "and then I shall go and fetch our dinner and bring it here and eat it with you, Comrade. Are you not hungry?"

I say, "Go now if you wish, Ma. You need not return soon. Stay close to the warmth of the boiling pots where they cook our dinner if you wish, Ma," I say, "I have no more duties for you to perform this night. I shall not devise the calligraphs this night." And I go outside to perform my duty at the camp's evening roll call.

I think to myself: Li, you have been a long time in this wretched place. It seems as if I have lived forever in this place! I ask myself: Li, shall you ever leave this place? It is as if I have always been here, that I shall always be here—the distant mountains shall always surround me, the cold and snow and wind of winter, the heat and drouth of summer, the turnip and bean fields that feed us, the deserted village of Yong Dong Po, the compound and the camp's latrines and huts and refuse pit, the prisoner corps of Negro and Caucasian Yankees, my comrades: Ma, Hong, Duc Fu, Soo . . . myself. I do not believe I shall ever leave this wretched place!

I try to remember: our triumphant columns of the heroic Volunteer Army crossing the Yalu, driving the armies of the Imperialist Yankees and their running dogs before us, the hordes of soldiers we captured at the Chosin Reservoir, the building of Prisoner Compound Number Nineteen.

I try to remember my days as a student at the People's Institute for Study of Alien Languages, Hangkow, my student comrades, the comrade teachers, the classroom recitations, the long hours of study, late into the nights, reading, memorizing glossary entries by the light of lamps so dim the delicate calligraphy of my Mandarin blurred on the page before me, the hard block alphabet of my English swam before my eyes! I try to remember the thrill of story, the music of poem—I try to remember my excitement at the call to arms in the service of People's War that took me away, across the Yalu to this place!

I try to remember my home and family, the city of Hangkow, my father and mother, brothers and sisters, their words and laughter, the warmth of our hearth, the steaming bowls of food on our table, the camaraderie of our talk as we discussed the history and glorious future of People's Revolution, how we gave ourselves together to the magnificent struggle, how we glowed like bright lamps with the fervor of our dedication, the truth of our idealism . . .

And though I remember these things, remember things we said, the faces of people, it is as if it is only a story, a legend told in a poem, a book, a fiction. It is as if the whole of my life is only a story, as if even People's War is only a story, like the novels of S. Crane and J. DeForest, as if all is only words, without sense or significance.

Li, I say to myself, who are you?

The night sky is black, and out of this blackness swirls a heavy snowfall that muffles the sound of my steps as I cross the compound, unseen by the sleepy sentries who stomp their feet, shield their faces from the snow with the upturned collars of their padded coats, sling their rifles across their backs to free their hands, tuck them under their armpits to warm them; the sleepy sentries do not see or hear me cross the compound.

I lean forward, trudge into the force of the wind that tears down from the distant mountains, the mountains lost in the blackness of the night, from which come only thick snow and the cutting wind. The sleepy sentries walk their posts, do not see or hear me pick my way past the latrines; it is too cold to smell the stench of the latrines. The sleepy sentries do not see me, do not hear me descend into the refuse pit, the ugly mounds of camp garbage concealed now, made white, lovely, by the snowfall.

The sleepy sentries, senses numbed with cold, do not detect me. Comrade Camp Commandant Duc Fu will be asleep, close to the warmth cast by the fire in his hut stove; does he dream of the Long March, of the caves of Hunan, his wounds, even as he sleeps in his warm hut? Comrade Soo will be asleep at this hour; does he dream of the writings of Comrades Marx and Engels, Lenin and Stalin, Mao and Chou, and Lin Piao, of slogans brushed on squares of rice paper? Hong sleeps with his comrades in their barracks hut; does he dream of arrogant

Yankee devils who torment him with vile words? Ma sleeps soundly, wrapped in the rags of his pallet on the earthen floor of my hut—will he dream of writing legible calligraphs in a ledger?

It is not until I am very close to the discarded caisson wheel that I hear their voices, so loud is the whip of the wind above the refuse pit, so thick the fall of snow in the air that it mutes their voices until I am very close to them.

"Mama," I hear Lester Boggs say.

"Shut to damn hell the fuck up, man!" I hear Raleigh Furman Smith say.

"Mama," says Lester Boggs. They do not seem to hear me, do not know I have come to be with them, even when I am very close, so close I can see their faces even in the snow-filled dark of this night.

Lester Boggs is almost covered by the snow; it lies over his feet and legs and torso, a gently curving drift. His arms and hands emerge from the drift, but even the ropes that bind him to the wheel are coated with the white snow. His face is veiled by snow that has gathered there, melted against his skin, re-frozen to a crystal mask in the bitter temperature of the wind. He docs not move, but his eyes blink, and his lips move, and he says only, "Mama."

"Will you fucking shut to fuck up!" says Raleigh Furman Smith. The snow coats him also, but he kicks his feet, twists his shoulders, as if he would snap the strong ropes that bind him to the wheel alongside Lester Boggs. He spits out snow-flakes that fall into his open mouth as he strains against the ropes that hold him.

"Lester," I say, and, "Raleigh Furman Smith, I, Li, come to be with you here in this place! Lester, do you comprehend me? Hello, Comrade Prisoner Smith!" I say.

"Mama," Lester Boggs says.

Raleigh Smith sees me now, looks at me; his face distorts, teeth bare, and he spits snowflakes from his lips before he speaks. "What the fuck you doing, man!" he says, and, "Li, man, you so fucking lame! You come to turn me aloose out of this shit, motherfucker? Fuck you doing, Li!"

"Wherefore you curse me?" I say, and, "I, Li, come here to you in this place. Do not villify, Raleigh Smith," I say, "as how I am come to expressing solidarities in durance you suffer. Do you not comprehend?"

"Mama," is all that Lester Boggs can say; he blinks, closes his eyes, as if he would now sleep.

"Motherfuck!" says Raleigh Smith. He thrashes, as if he would kick at me, closes his eyes, clenches his jaw, looks away into the blackness of the night, the falling snow that covers us. I kneel in the snow before them, take great care to choose my English words before I speak.

"Comrades," I say, and, "Lester Boggs. Raleigh Smith. I did decree this durance in service of high causes. This I did. You said vile words, contrary to good orders and disciplines, Geneva Convention. This is so, Lester!"

"Mama," Lester says. He does not open his eyes. I do not see his lips move to speak.

"Raleigh Smith," I say, "I did prevaricate. This I did. Done is done, Raleigh!"

"Man, jive shit," he says, and, "You killing us, Jim!"

"Perhaps," I say, and, "Probables," and, "I am he who loves words, do you comprehend? Mandarin," I say, and, "English. I did prevaricate. Thus, hence, I come here in confessional, also in sincere integrity of actions to redeem false utterances. Do you comprehend me, Comrades?"

"Mama," Lester Boggs says.

"Motherfucker killing our ass!" screams Raleigh Furman Smith, and, "We dying, man! Dying fucking dead!"

"Listen, Comrades! Hear!" I say, but cannot find the words I would say. I would say to them: Comrades, I, Li, am such a one as you! We are but men, beasts gifted with speech. I, Li, am a lover of words, a student of my Mandarin and your English. I love even the obscenities of your argot! I betray my life with the lie I told, Raleigh Furman Smith! I did condemn you to death by freezing in this place, Lester! I am come here to be with you, to share your suffering in solidarity, redeem the lie I told, redeem all the words I have spoken, redeem what I love, myself . . .

I say, "I speak to you belly to heart," and, "Such an end is not foreseen, as in fictions of W. Porter, than which who employs name of Henry, O., is this not oddness of life and languages?"

"Mama," I think I hear Lester Boggs say.

"Fucking jive shit jive," says Raleigh Smith; he thrashes at me with his feet, will not look at me.

"You comprehend not, Comrades," I say. And I say no more. I wish that words might come to me, that I might speak with them of who and what I am, that they might tell me of themselves, of the places called Stillwater, in Oklahoma, and Detroit, and I might tell them of my city of Hangkow. But my words will not come to me—the wind is too loud, the snow so thick, the cold so intense it stiffens my tongue when I open my mouth to speak. Lester Boggs speaks no more; it is as if he has fallen fast asleep. I do not listen to the cursing of Raleigh Furman Smith.

I kneel before them, unmoving, bound fast to this place with them by my pledge, stronger than any vow I might take in words. I do not seek for words to tell them how we are together in the cold and snow and dark of this place.

The Parts of Speech

I tell myself that a healthy imagination is like a healthy appetite
and must be fed. If you do not feed it the lives of your friends, I
maintain, then you are apt to feed it your own life, to live in your
imagination rather than upon it.

— Peter Taylor, *Daphne's Lover*

I am a writer, a man who makes fictions. I take things, real
things—people, events, language—and I make them into fictions. I take the real people I know or have known, and what
happens to them, and what they say to me, or what I have
heard them say to others, and to one another, and I think about
all this, and sometimes, when I am working well, I am able to
make real people's lives into fictions that are more real than
what I began with. Sometimes I am not able to achieve this,
and there is no fiction, and the real people and their lives remain just that—real. When they do not become fictions, I forget them as soon as I can, and I go on to the next people, their
lives, their words, the next fiction.

Making fictions is a craft, and a writer is a craftsman. He
needs skills to practice his craft successfully; the skills can be
learned if he works hard. And he also needs something besides

skills. Some people call this *talent*, what the writer needs in addition to the skills he can learn by working hard and using his imagination. I do not know what *talent* is. I do not call it *talent*. I do not know what to call it, this other thing the writer needs. But it exists; it is there. I use it all the time when I make fictions out of all the real people and lives and words I have experienced in my life.

I do not worry that I have no name for this quality that enables people to be writers, make fictions. Though I do think a lot about it. And sometimes I am not entirely certain it is a wholly good thing. Which is not to say I have any doubts about the value of fiction. I am a writer, and I love writing, and I love fictions and fictionmaking. There are times I wish I could love it unreservedly, without any doubt about what it is a writer uses besides his skills and his imagination to make real people into fictions.

This is a story, in three parts, about myself, and about my being a writer, and about the way I make my fictions. The first two parts of this story are true, as accurate as my memory will permit; the last part is not. The whole of it is a story, a fiction.

In 1954, when I was sixteen, my family moved from the east side of the city of Milwaukee to its far west side, to the suburb of Wauwatosa. So I transferred from Riverside High School to Wauwatosa Senior High School to begin my junior year.

Like many adolescents, my response to my daily agony of self-consciousness was to present a studied, intense façade of jaded indifference to everyone—my parents, my teachers, the other students, who seemed to me to occupy received positions of security and self-confidence so firm that nothing could ever shake the suburban foundations of their juvenile social orders. I was struck dumb, near panic, by their seemingly effortless competence in classes, their ease in the organized busywork of clubs and sports, the subtle, rich flux of their sexual pairings, innocent, but spiced with unknown hints of permissiveness, casual sophistication, the occasional serious romance.

In short, a stranger, a trite and stereotypical outsider, awkward and boorish, a touch homely, ambitious and timid, cunning and ignorant, paralyzed by the tension between my natural dreams of popularity and the fact of my obvious inconsequentiality, between the necessary vision of my special individuality and the dull certainty of how ordinary I was, I withdrew inward.

To the world—parents, teachers, peers—I offered a stony and stoic indifference bordering on perfunctory hostility. Inwardly, I seethed, so deliberately sensitive I registered nuances like a psychological seismograph. To the world, I showed myself a rock of placidity, emotionally dormant, on occasion skeptically, cynically observant, rarely puzzled, almost never interested. Inside myself, where I could live, was chaos; my thoughts raged with contradictions, my eyes dazzled by the strobe-flash opacity of life around me, ears numbed by its din, flesh and feeling a riot of puberty's multiplying cells, my inner voice an unbroken shriek, the whole of me perpetually churned by my frenetic glands.

My ethos, if I could be said to have had one at age sixteen, in 1954, was: I see, but am not seen; I hear, but do not speak; I know, but am unknown.

My routine was to arrive at school late enough each day to miss the clusters of students gathered near the main doors to tease and gossip until the final tardy warning bell rang; while they jostled and flirted, their voices carrying to me like the taunt of sirens on the clear early morning air, I lurked angrily behind someone's maroon Ford hotrod in the student parking lot, smoking a last bitter cigarette, poised to spring when the bell clanged its inevitable gloomy summons.

In the crowded, noisy halls, I threaded my way to my locker like some preoccupied commuter; as I opened the combination lock, threw my gray, anonymous jacket on the hook, found the textbooks I would need for the day, I shot furtive glances at the girls who took time for a last primp in the mirrors hung on the insides of their locker doors, the excessively jocular boys who shouted across heads to one another, traded mock-punches, slammed their locker doors shut, snapped locks in place.

I might as well have been invisible, watching sidelong and silent from the shadowy nook where chance—for once in my favor—had assigned my locker.

I slipped into my homeroom with great skill, never among the first to enter and take my chosen seat—in the last row, of course, back to the wall—never the last, always shielded within the median and mode, that stumbling group, the majority, who funneled in together, spread out to their seats as though by osmosis. In my seat, I assumed my obligatory slouch behind the stained and nicked desk, elbows braced on its surface, head propped against my hands, as if shading my eyes from the window's dusty sunlight—as if I nursed a migraine or hangover headache, as if I meant to doze through the first half-hour of the morning, as if I had drawn an opaque, impenetrable bubble about myself.

Inscrutable, thus impervious, I took in the sensations that played about me in homeroom class, absorbed them the way a sponge might take on water splashed randomly against it.

I listened to the rustle of my classmates' clothing as they fidgeted at their desks—the crackle of crisp shirts and blouses, shuffle of shoes on the scuffed wooden floor, the whispered slide of legs crossing, uncrossing. I listened: click-click of ballpoint pens, rip and rustle of notebook paper, dry slap of books opened and closed, the rattle and ring of bracelets, the tedious rhythm of long sighs, muffled giggles, sotto voce exchanges, a snort, coughing. From the front of the room, Miss Myrna Klemp, Latin teacher, our homeroom monitor, cleared her throat daintily as prelude to calling the roll.

The morning sunlight from the windows fell on me like a warm bath, and I smelled the odors generated in the room by its accumulating heat: the flat, dry smell of the wooden floors mixed with the oily tinge of the janitor's sweeping compound, spiced with the worn varnish on desktops; the powdered scent of chalk, blackboards, chalktrays; the day's first perspiration blunted by a melange of flowery perfumes and colognes; the residue of cigarettes on my fingers.

Peering out from the tunnel of my cupped hands, my eyes moved from the scruffy, pimpled back of the neck of the boy seated directly in front of me to the embryonic sideburns being cultured by the boy to his left, the wispy tendril of a loosening spitcurl floating beneath the pearly ear of the girl to his right, the impossibly broad shoulders of an athlete, straining his lettersweater, the exact bas-relief of a fat girl's brassiere.

I considered—and dismissed—my classmates as Miss Myrna Klemp chirped their names in alphabetical order: Ardith Anne Allen (fat girl with enormous breasts, rigid brassiere, too much jewelry, her lilac scent a purple miasma hovering about her, left behind in her wake) . . . Sidney Brodson (only Jew in the junior class) . . . William Fifer (candy eater, cheeks always swollen with suck-hards, flecks of licorice between his dingy teeth, in the corners of his sticky lips) . . . Sue Gralman (most popular, unfailingly cheerful, greets even me with a toothy slash of a smile, waves at everyone in her field of vision, both *nice* and *cute*, thus hateful) . . . Leonard Leff, Jr. (president of the Foto Club, Leica suspended on a strap from his neck, gadget bag on his hip, totes a tripod, distracted, smug in his technical competence) . . . Oscar Southard (considered *dirty*, shunned by all girls and many of the boys because he swears, carries a condom pressed in his shabby wal-

let, delights in sharing his obscene picturebooks) . . . Melinda
Tate (so spectacularly beautiful no boy dares approach her,
reputed to date college men, uses a sunlamp to maintain a per-
petual Florida tan the exact shade of breakfast waffles, a supe-
rior creature beyond even my scorn) . . . Geoffrey Walker
(class brain, a shoo-in for valedictorian, vain and pompous,
utterly devoid of physical grace, winner of regional science
fair competitions, almost as friendless as I) . . . Eduardo
Walkiewicz (brutish, a hulking football player and wrestler,
child of a Mexican mother, Polish father, his swarthy face pos-
sesses a cunningly Oriental cast that contradicts his unmitigated
stupidity) . . . Jeanmarie Young (notorious slut, an untouch-
able) . . . Mary Helen Zimmerman (very short haircut, darkly
haired forearms and calves, incipient moustache, suspected of
liking girls more than boys) . . .

Some say *present*, some say *here*; when Miss Myrna
Klemp calls my name I respond with a contemptuous grunt,
like the grumpy protest of a hibernating animal disturbed out
of season in its cave.

And so it was, schoolday after schoolday—the weekends
and holidays my only reprieves—that I coped with, survived
both the upsetting move to Wauwatosa Senior High School in
my junior year and the excruciating burlesque of adolescent
self-consciousness I inflicted upon myself when I was sixteen,
in 1954.

Moved from homeroom to first-hour class, from first-hour
to second, class to class throughout the day by clammering
schoolbells, I wove my way through the jammed halls, up and
down the thundering wooden stairs, never bumping, brushing,
never touching, never touched.

In American History, I retired behind my massive textbook, let Mr. Rollins' flow of comment on current events (Joe
McCarthy was still a celebrity), relieved by personal anecdotes
from his experience in World War II, slide around and over

me while I read and reread a paragraph, or simply stared at the page until the words blurred, Mr. Rollins' voice became a husky buzz. In Solid Geometry, Mrs. Cook scarce knew I existed; her back to us, intent on the constructs she chalked on the smeared chalkboard, she struggled with truncated cones and parallelograms, pyramids and rhomboids, while I doodled on my graph paper. In German class—an alternative to Miss Myrna Klemp's Latin—I sat up straight for Frau Rognebakke, loaned my reluctant voice to the class chorus as we bent our throats to repeat her umlaut sounds, chanted the conjugations of irregular verbs. I enjoyed Geography, received my best grades from Mr. Warren, who loved maps, and so appreciated the clean lines I drew in colored inks to limn the borders of states and nations, the meanderings of great world rivers. There was no threat in Art Appreciation; in good weather, Mrs. Pixton took us outdoors to sketch. It was appropriate for me to take shelter behind a tree to scratch out the shape of the school's towers against the sky with a soft pencil—I varied the cloud pattern, always added a bird or two in flight, suggested the off-the-page sun with planes of shading. And in Physical Education, Harold "Wristlock" Mathias, rumored to have been an NCAA wrestling champion at Oklahoma A & M in the impossibly distant 1930s, was content as long as each boy generated at least a visible film of perspiration; he considered team sports and games unmasculine, so allowed us to *work out*, as he called it, individually. Often, I did lazy sit-ups. When no mats or weights or punching bags were free, I escaped by jogging slowly around the gym floor perimeter, picking up my pace whenever I felt Wristlock Mathias watching me, hands on hips, torso still muscled under his tight white tee-shirt, shaking his head in resigned disgust at the flabby, indifferent generation I exemplified. In Chemistry, since Mr. Davis did not trust us to use chemicals, I could perch on a table at the rear of the laboratory to watch him create chlorine gas under a bell jar or gingerly transfer a lump of sodium from a can of kerosene to a tub of water to demonstrate its volatility. I passed his course by memorizing the Periodic Table of Atomic Elements. So I coped, survived. My stance and my strategies worked, and no one—my parents, teachers, fellow students—challenged me. Except in my English class, taught by Miss Agnes Keintzle, who began each class with a drill designed to compel us to demonstrate a thorough knowledge of the parts of speech. It was a large class, at least thirty students. The most remote seat I could find was the second-last in the row next to the windows, where I could bask, dormant, in the mote-filled late afternoon sunlight that fell into the stuffy room, ignore the teacher, think my own twisting thoughts, observe, as anonymous as I was in German or Chemistry or Solid Geometry.

Miss Agnes Keintzle was notoriously undemanding, never assigned essays to be written outside class, her homework assignments calling only for short readings in the anthology of excerpts from English and American literary classics that was our text, expected no one to venture any opinion about poetry or fiction or drama, never asked anyone to speculate as to the relationship of literature to life or other potentially embarrassing subjects. She loved her students, knew them all well, called them by their first names, had taught most of them as freshmen and sophomores, was universally popular because she seldom gave a grade lower than B. The only matter on which she took an unshakeable stand was the parts of speech.

She began her classes with a drill on the parts of speech. Thereafter, she chattered about the day's reading assignment, the form of the ballad stanza, the characteristics of tragic heroes, the symbolic ambiguity of Hester's scarlet letter. On occasion, she read passages aloud with no more than a minimally silly injection of feeling interpretation; rarely, she asked open questions to test our reading, counting on her reliables, a claque of sycophantic girls and Geoffrey Walker, the class brain, to answer promptly, fully, and accurately.

I was, I thought, safe. I could, I thought, warm myself in the sunlight, muse, watch, read at random in the textbook, doodle in the margins. Survive. But there was no refuge from her parts of speech drill. It was a convenient substitute for calling the roll, and it was her sole pedagogic passion, the one body of finite information she had taken to her heart, determined to impart to the generations of students who passed through her charge, semester after semester. And she succeeded in this, if only by the inexorable pressure of routine, embedding this knowledge in her students, as if her drills on the parts of speech were a perpetually renewed drop of water that imperceptibly wore away the rock of our ignorance.

Agnes Keintzle was a merry, bouncy woman, always smiling—the shine of her too-white, too-even dentures struck me as predatory; her too-red lipstick matched the glossy polish on her talon-length nails; she wore expensive clothes, too-young fashions color coordinated with the purse that sat on her desk, her high-heel pumps that cracked on the wooden floors as she moved about in front of the class, conducting her drill on the parts of speech; her hair was always set in an elaborate coiffure, glinting, a hopelessly artificial, metallic platinum, no strand out of place; her watery eyes were magnified by thick lenses set in flamboyant bows, secured by a garish ribbon around her neck; the peach shade of pancake on her cheeks and forehead contrasted with the raised, dark veins in the backs of her hands, the ropy muscles dancing in her forearms, the trembling crepe of her throat.

I feared her, knew I was not safe in her classroom, that junior English would expose me—to her, the other students, myself. As she brought out her flashcards, slipped the wide rubberband off the pack, I tightened myself against disaster, hunched deeper in my seat.

Her voice veered back and forth between a girl's lilt and a crone's croak. I tried to will myself dead. "Everybody ready?" she asked. "Everybody alert today? Here we go, class!"

She drilled us on the parts of speech. She had been drilling my classmates as freshmen, sophomores, so they were ready. They knew her, knew the drill, had responded for two years to the same worn pack of flashcards, memorized the correct answers, could call out accurate responses as readily as I might spit in a gutter to express feigned disgust. They lifted their heads, squared their shoulders, sat up; they were ready, and I was not.

"Why do we do this, class?" she asked. "Because it teaches us what we have to know if we want to know our language, doesn't it. And we all know our language is the most marvelous tool for living we have, don't we. Because it's very, very precise, and it's also flexible, so we can take that precision and adopt it for anything we need, can't we. Because we know it's not an instinct, like an animal barking. It's not a mystery, is it. And if you can say what you want to you can achieve anything you set out after, can't you."

The class looked at her; some returned her stiff smile, some nodded. And when she had finished telling them—as she had told them when they were freshmen, sophomores—of the flexible precision of language that would enable them to be and do whatever they chose in life, and how the parts of speech were solid little foundation building blocks—they could think of punctuation marks as little fasteners that held the parts of speech together in sentences—that all this, if mastered, would lead them to successful careers and satisfying lives, she began her drill. Easy in their familiarity with her false, bubbling enthusiasm, easy in their collective sense of themselves, the certitude of who and where and when they were, they began. They stood her drill on the parts of speech with a communal tone of security so alien to me it might have been a formal dialogue in a foreign tongue, a rite performed in an ancient religion, a game played on Mars.

"Now," Miss Agnes Keintzle said, and took the first card from the pack, held it above her head, waved it like a semaphore flag. Starting with the first seat in the first row, nearest the door, she proceeded. Down that row in order, front to back, to the first seat, second row, down that row, to the first seat, third row, Agnes Keintzle flashed her cards, snapped her glistening dentures in approval as each student in turn gave the correct answer.

And I sat hunched at my desk, watching the inevitable approach of her attention to the last row, second-last seat, the irresistible march of the parts of speech toward me.

I was not ready, knew I could not do it. At Riverside High School, we had not studied the parts of speech. As a freshman, I was required to read *Julius Caesar* and *Silas Marner*, to write synoptic book reports that I do not recall were ever evaluated, no grade assigned until the perfunctory end-of-semester C. In my sophomore year we read some poetry and *The Merchant of Venice*, and I earned a B by matching quoted lines and passages of dialogue with the names of poets and Shakespeare's characters.

I was ignorant of the parts of speech. I was ignorant of grammar, of punctuation, could no more diagram a sentence than I could have delivered a discourse on formal rhetoric.

I was not ready; I was ignorant, laughably so, and when Agnes Keintzle reached me with her flashcards, she would know it, all my classmates would know it, and the stance and strategies of withdrawal that were my way of living as a transfer student in the junior class at Wauwatosa Senior High School in 1954, when I was sixteen, would be destroyed. I would have no way of living, no way to survive, to be who and where and when I was.

Of course I had known about her drills before I entered her class. I knew a great deal, eavesdropping, about teachers, classes, other students at Wauwatosa Senior High School. So I knew it would happen before it happened, but did not really believe it would happen—like most teenagers, the only true reality for me was the immediate, excruciating present, the moment I occupied in time and space. Yesterday was a figment of memory, tomorrow a shifting, unreliable rumor.

Agnes Keintzle gave the first week of class over to organization and orientation, the second to lectures on the vital significance and seductively interesting nature of language arts studies, though she did mention what she intended, and why, for the parts of speech. It was only in the third week, a Tuesday, that it came to pass. Memory and rumor merged to create the present, and I sat, hunched, waiting for it to happen to me as it happened.

Down and down and down the rows of desks she went. Everyone was confident, competent.

"Ardith?" said Miss Keintzle, waggling the flashcard at her: *school*. And fat Ardith Anne Allen smirked, drew her enormous breasts up in a deep breath, said, "Noun. Also it can be a verb if you say like for example, *He was schooled in Latin*."

"Excellent," said Agnes Keintzle. "And that's a common noun when it's a noun, isn't it, Ardith." She tucked the card in at the back of the deck, flashed the next off the top: *Milwaukee*.

"Proper noun," said the girl seated behind Ardith Anne.

"Excellent. Which functions to?"

"Name a particular person, place, or thing."

"Fine. Next?" *Drove*.

"Verb."

"What kind?"

"Transitive."

"Used in a sentence?"

"He drove his car to the game. Or, he drove the golf ball far," said Leonard Leff, Jr.

"Perfect. Billy?" *Is*. William Fifer swallowed the juice of whatever confection he was eating, pushed it to one side of his mouth with his tongue, wiped his wet lips on his sleeve, answered that it was a linking verb, used it correctly in a sentence.

Down and down the rows went Agnes Keintzle. Verbs; the

properties of verbs (tense, mood, voice, transitive-intransitive, linking, verbals, participles, gerunds, infinitives); adjectives (positive, comparative, superlative); adverbs (those changing form to indicate comparison, those which cannot); prepositions; conjunctions. Row by row, seat by seat. Sue Gralman simpered over a conjunctive adverb; Oscar Southard leered wickedly, stumbled on a relative pronoun, recovered almost immediately; Melinda Tate's serenity was unaffected by the challenge of creating a set of grammatical equivalents on either side of *but*. Even Eduardo Walkiewicz, eyes blank as a statue's, was able to haltingly join a subordinate adverbial clause to the main clause of a sentence with *because*. Class brain Geoffrey Walker was ludicrously untested by an interjection.

And then Agnes Keintzle reached me with her flashcards. I do not remember which card Miss Keintzle held up for me. It did not, does not matter. My ignorance of the parts of speech was such that she might as well have asked me to translate a calligraph or a rune; I only remember sitting, frozen, time in that moment frozen, seeing Agnes Keintzle, the smile of her feral dentures, red smear of her lipstick, matching nails clutching the card aloft, the platinum helmet of her hairdo, her gelatinous eyes bright behind her magnifying spectacles.

I was frozen, paralyzed—there was no movement of time, no sound I heard, as if some translucent screen separated me from Agnes Keintzle, the cryptic card she held up for me to see, the rows and ranks of students who seemed caught in suspended animation, waiting until something happened to bring us all, everything, back to motion, sound, life. I do not know how long this moment of horrible stasis might have lasted.

What happened, what saved me, was the correct response, the answer whispered from behind me, from the last seat in my row, whispered in my ear by Cynthia von Eschen, the girl who sat behind me in Miss Agnes Keintzle's junior English class at Wauwatosa Senior High School, in 1954.

I do not remember the answer she whispered—only the

perfect, clear, soft quality of her voice, so faint, yet as distinct as if it were my own articulate thought. And I knew, was absolutely certain in the instant I heard her whisper, that no one else in the classroom could hear her. It was totally unexpected, unhoped for, a miracle—I sat, frozen on the edge of disaster; Cynthia von Eschen whispered the correct answer to me; I repeated it, loud, emphatic; Agnes Keintzle said *excellent* or *fine* or *very good*, or she tightened her fierce smile a notch, put away her flashcards, took up a poem or a novel excerpt from our text. And it was over, and I was safe again, safe forever, could live as I had to live, then and there and thereafter.

I did not, do not understand what happened, why. I had never paid the slightest attention, taken the slightest notice of Cynthia von Eschen, would not have known her name, perhaps not even recognized her in the halls before that day she saved me.

From my withdrawn stance I had considered—and rejected—the students in my homeroom: Ardith Anne Allen's obesity, surrounded by the wall of her lilac scent, bovine breasts straining her blouse, was a pathetic fat girl who vainly sought femininity; Sidney Brodson was a Jew, doomed to the isolation of inarticulate prejudice; William Fifer's candy addiction rendered him childlike, hopelessly immature; Sue Gralman's programmed affability was patently bogus, a naked social politics; Leonard Leff, Jr.'s Leica and gadget bag defined his own inscrutable, eccentric space; Oscar Southard's nasty fascination with filth enabled anyone to feel a tangible moral superiority; Melinda Tate's beauty was quite simply otherworldly, no more real than a painting or a photograph; Geoffrey Walker's straight-A grades were beneath contempt; Eduardo Walkiewicz's crude bulk and blatantly slow mind made it almost possible to pity him, his athletic prowess only minimally mitigating; the reputed sexual extremity and perversity of Jeanmarie Young and Mary Helen Zimmerman cast them both outside the pale of conventional decency.

There was no one I noticed from within the fastness of my self-imposed alienation, no one with whom I was thrown together in homeroom or classes, from whom I could not distance myself. But I had never noticed Cynthia von Eschen, and it took an effort to do so after she had saved me in the parts of speech drill.

I did not speak to her that day in class, did not thank her for what she had done for me when we were at last dismissed by the raucous bell. But I did, from my sullen remove, now observe, take notice of her—in the halls, taking my seat in English class before she reached hers behind me, remaining there when the bell dismissed us, watching her leave the room.

Cynthia von Eschen was surely the plainest, least remarkable girl in the junior class. She moved about so unobtrusively, spoke so seldom, greeting only when greeted, she might have been only the shadow of her plain substance; she appeared to embody, as naturally as light or air or motion itself, the impenetrable anonymity I made for myself through unblinking alertness and unstinting effort.

Cynthia von Eschen wore her pale brown hair in a short ponytail, just a little out of fashion—junior and senior girls had begun to blaze peroxide streaks back from their hairlines, to frame their faces in white-frosted tips, to clip their manes, shave the backs of their necks in gamin cuts. She wore glasses, of course, but not the thick, distorting lenses of a Miss Keintzle or the harlequin frames, so recently popular, that her peers sucked on coyly as much as they wore them; her lenses were small and round—they seemed to constrict her face, pinch her small eyes even closer together. She wore no makeup that I could see, her brows unplucked, her thin lips bloodless, no earrings, no rings on her fingers, her skin white enough to show light blue veins at her temples, her wrists. Her nails were a washed dull white with large, whiter halfmoons, trimmed blunt. She was thin, her flat chest absurd in contrast with the cone-breasts most girls flaunted. Her dresses were buttoned to the last button, dowdy when seen against the cashmere sweaters and teasing cleavages popular then, the hobble skirts that stressed the fullness of thighs and calves. Her legs were sticks, and she did not affect the conventional posture, one crossed over the other, foot bouncing seductively as Agnes Keintzle droned on about language and literature. Cynthia von Eschen skittered in and out of English class, her steps mincing, as if her slightly too-large feet had been bound from infancy. She stood and walked slump-shouldered, clutching her books and ringbinder to her bony chest, as if they were a shield, armored her against any accidental encounter. Her eyes, tiny behind her pinching spectacles, were always down, as if measuring her tiny steps or counting the tiles, memorizing the pattern of the floorboards.

Cynthia von Eschen was the plainest, most unattractive, most inconsequential girl in the junior class at Wauwatosa Senior High School in 1954, and I had not a grain of curiosity or interest in her, but she knew the parts of speech as well as even Geoffrey Walker, and she whispered my answers to me, day after day, all through that semester, spared me—for a reason or reasons I cannot know—the shame that would, without her rescue, have destroyed me, as I was, the year I was sixteen years old.

She saved me, day after day, week after week, through the semester. Miss Agnes Keintzle grinned her terrible grin, flashed her cards, seat by seat, row by row. Noun and pronoun, verbs transitive and intransitive, verbs expressing the qualities of tense, mood, and voice, linking verbs and verbals, participles, gerund and infinitive, adjectives and adverbs, positive, comparative, and superlative, prepositions, coordinating and correlative conjunctions, conjunctive adverbs, subordinating conjunctions, relative pronouns, interjections—which, Agnes Keintzle never failed to remind us, were generally to be avoided in formal writing.

We drilled the parts of speech, and, always, Cynthia von Eschen's clear whisper sounded in my ear alone, the correct answer; I almost began to think I was actually learning, coming to master the parts of speech, that Cynthia von Eschen's delicate whisper was only a confirmation of my growing expertise. And the semester ended, and I received a final grade of C+ from Miss Keintzle, and I passed to another teacher, another class for the second semester of junior English, and I was never again in a class with Cynthia von Eschen, but it did not matter because no other English teacher at Wauwatosa Senior High School seemed to care about the parts of speech, those finite foundation building blocks of our marvelous, precise, and flexible language.

I never thanked Cynthia von Eschen for what she had done for me. I never turned in my seat just before or after class began to say thank you to her. I never caught her outside the door, before or after class, to say thank you. I never stopped her on the rare occasions when we happened to pass in the crowded halls, never thanked her. We never shared another class, but I saw her two or three times a week for the next year and a half. I stood close to her in the line of graduates, dressed in our gray gowns and mortarboards, as we marched through the auditorium to the stage, paced by the organ rendition of "Pomp and Circumstance," in June of 1955—the last time I saw Cynthia von Eschen. And I did not speak to her, never thanked her.

Why did she do it? I cannot know that. Like the parts of speech, it was a mystery I did not care to solve. Pity? Kindness? Did she, perhaps, from within her mousy inconsequentiality, express some boy–girl interest in me? I can never know the answer to this.

I simply did not care, then. I sat back in my impregnable stance, watching and listening—contemplating the big breasts of Ardith Anne Allen, the infuriating, self-serving camaraderie of Sue Gralman, the unattainable beauty of Melinda Tate, the sluttish allure of Jeanmarie Young. I never learned why Cynthia von Eschen came to my rescue, and I did not care, then. It is now that I think about this, often. But I can never know the answer or answers. Who I was then, who she was—the *then* of then, this is always a mystery, and memory only invokes it, never answers or resolves.

———•———

This is the first part of my story. Here is the second part, the shortest of the three I promised; it is also true.

———•———

In 1965 I lived in New York and received an invitation, forwarded from my parents' address, to attend the first reunion of Wauwatosa Senior High School's class of 1955. It was impossible for me to travel a thousand miles; I was very busy becoming a writer of fictions. So I wrote Susan Hackett (née Gralman), class secretary—the payoff for her unremitting effort to ingratiate herself with everyone. I wrote to her and said I was becoming a writer of fictions now, unable to attend. I sent a check for three dollars, so that I would receive the information-packed souvenir directory that would be published, that would tell me all about my former classmates, where they had gone, what, who they had become in the ten years since graduation.

I thought no more about it. Weeks passed, the reunion was held, but I had forgotten about it. When, several months later, the souvenir booklet arrived, bent, the envelope tattered, I read it. It gave the names, addresses, occupations of all my former classmates, and I was surprised at how few of the names I recognized, how little I cared about where they had gone in life, what they had become. It was interesting only because some of them ran so true to form, while others seemed to have defied all the laws of probability.

Ardith Anne Allen had become Ardith Anne Zucker, was one of four graduates with four children; a prize was given at the reunion to a girl named Gail Speer (née Gooch), who, with five, had the most children. I did not remember Gail Gooch, but could imagine Ardith Anne Allen nursing her infants with ease. Sidney Brodson was married, two children, very successful in banking and insurance, prominent in the Anti-Defamation League. Melinda Tate had, of course, married well, the heir to Milwaukee's Gettleman Brewery. Geoffrey Walker had earned a doctorate in physics at the University of Wisconsin, was already an associate professor at Penn State, listed publications concerning research on laser beam applications. The order of these destinies, governing logic, was clear.

But William Fifer, who also failed to attend, was listed as a television weatherman for one of the major Chicago stations. Oscar Southard had graduated from Purdue, then founded his own engineering consulting firm in California. Leonard Leff, Jr., owned and operated a Phillips 66 station on Milwaukee's south side. Sue Gralman Hackett was twice-divorced. Jeanmarie Young had attended college, married, had a child, was a successful part-time Avon lady; she described herself as a contented homemaker. Eduardo Walkiewicz listed himself as employed by the Wauwatosa Municipal Sanitation Department, made no mention of having gone on to college football or wrestling. I found no logic—only wonder, the suggestion of mystery—in these new identities.

And there was a description of the dinner dance held at the Pfister Hotel's ballroom, the professional master of ceremonies who awarded the prizes: for the woman (née Gooch) with the most children, the man with the least hair, the fattest man, the graduate who traveled the greatest distance to attend (a career Air Force officer on furlough from his post in Alaska), the most famous (William Fifer, television weatherman). There was mention of the teachers who came, but neither Myrna Klemp nor Agnes Keintzle was among them—I thought of the parts of speech.

And there was a short necrology, on the inside back cover of the booklet, like an afterthought—that, in addition to all these life-changes, higher education, occupations, careers, marriages, children, travel, there was, lest we forget, one more, greater, final change.

There were six people listed, six of the more than four hundred graduates of Wauwatosa Senior High School, class of 1955, who had died during the preceding ten years. Of the six, I recognized only the name of Cynthia von Eschen.

I read her name on the list of the dead, and I thought of her, remembered her, Miss Keintzle's class, the parts of speech. I remembered all that very clearly, and I am sure it was sad to think she was dead, but I could not really imagine it.

A little over a year later, I went back to Wisconsin to visit my parents. I borrowed my father's car and drove about the city of Milwaukee, the suburb of Wauwatosa, past the high school, and it was purely by chance that I met Eduardo Walkiewicz.

I stopped behind a municipal sanitation truck, and there he was, emptying a trashcan into the dumpster; I did not recognize him at first, he had gained so much weight, his overalls and gloves so dirty, his black hair shot with premature grey. Then I recognized him, and after only an instant's satisfaction at seeing him—what, who he was now—I leaned my head out of the car window, called to him, and he came over, leaned on the car, spoke with me for a minute before he had to go, follow his truck to the next house on its route.

I am not sure why I called out to him.

I smelled the sour stench of garbage on his clothes as we spoke. I mentioned the reunion, and he told me who he remembered seeing there. He had been most surprised at what had happened to Sue Gralman; with three children, twice-divorced, she subsisted on Aid to Dependent Children, welfare, foodstamps; he remembered her as such a nice girl in high school, friendly. I mentioned seeing Cynthia von Eschen's name among the dead, and said I wondered how she had died. He had talked with someone at the reunion who knew the story of her death. And he told it to me, a brief sketch, before his driver honked, shifted the truck's gears, and Eduardo Walkiewicz followed on foot after the truck to the next house on the garbage collection route.

***

What follows, the last part of my story, is not true; it is a fiction I have made out of two sources, what Eduardo Walkiewicz, the garbage collector, told me that day, and from my fiction writer's imagination. What he told me was already a kind of unselfconscious fiction, a fabric of the truth so remote from the experience it related as to be wholly unreliable, passed through at least two unreliable, incompetent sensibilities—Eduardo Walkiewicz and whoever told him what he told me. And my imagination is only remotely tied to whatever facts came to me; I have my own reasons for making the kind of fiction that follows, and even the best intention has to be manifest in words. I take everything I know, everything I am, have been, and I have to use words, and the words are the fiction, what follows.

***

Henry Peña was born and raised in the Santa Fe *barrio*. The youngest of seven children, he was small and sickly as a child, skinny and weak as an adolescent, and the most notorious liar in the *barrio*.

When he was seven, he told his best friend, Luis Roybal,

that his true father was not the man who lived with his mother; his true father, he told Luis, was a rich man from Old Mexico, a *patron*, who had come across the border just long enough to father him, then gone back to his *rancho* where he raised racehorses and fighting bulls, and someday soon he would come back to Santa Fe to find Henry, take him back to Old Mexico to live with him.

"You lie, Henry. You always lie. I heard your mother say to my mother your father was this guy from Clovis lived with her until then you were born. Why you always lie, Henry?"

"It could as easy be my mother telling lies, Luis," Henry said.

"Except it ain't," his friend said. "Henry, you the worst big liar I ever know. Hey, if you got to tell lies, make something people already don't know the truth about, maybe then somebody believe you, hey?"

When he was fourteen, Henry stole change from his mother's purse, bought a bottle of blue-black ink, borrowed one of her sewing needles, and tattooed *Pachuko* crosses between the thumb and forefinger of both his hands. He kept his hands in his pockets until the swelling went down and the tattoos scabbed off. Then he showed them to Luis Roybal. He told him, "Man, you see this bad crosses? Means I am *Pachuko*, see? I join up with these bad dudes, you don't know them, Luis, they not from the *barrio*, see? Really bad they are, man. Now I belong, anybody messes with me, I give them the word, man, *Pachuko* all come, even from as far as Los Angeles if I say, kill anybody messes with Henry Peña, see? Same for me, I gang up on anybody bothers my *Pachuko* brothers, see?"

Luis Roybal said, "Henry, you done that yourself with a needle. Man, everybody know, your sister saying she seen you poking ink in your skin with a needle, man. You a damn liar ever since I know you, man!"

"No, honest, I'm telling you, I join up with the *Pachuko*, man! It's true. We the toughest people in Santa Fe, Luis!"

"The only place you tough is in your mouth always lying," Luis said. "And so where's your knife? *Pachuko* is always got a big knife, no? You don't even got no knifes! Liar Henry is your name, man!"

Of course he lied about having women too, but everybody did that, even Luis Roybal.

When he was seventeen, he joined the army with his friend Luis Roybal. He said to his mother, "We will be paratroopers. You get to wear shiny boots all the time, and the pay is extra because it's so dangerous to jump out of airplanes with only a parachute, see? Paratroopers is the most dangerous and toughest soldiers in the whole damn army, Mama!"

That was not supposed to be a lie, because he and Luis did enlist for airborne training. Luis was accepted, and went off to Fort Campbell, Kentucky, to join the Special Forces, but Henry Peña was rejected, found physically fit only for conventional duty. He took basic training at Fort Leonard Wood, Missouri, failed the advanced infantry training test, and was sent to Fort Riley, Kansas, assigned to Headquarters Quartermaster Company of the 1st Division.

His duty consisted of spending every Monday taking in all of division headquarters' dirty sheets; on Tuesdays he shook out all the dirty sheets and folded them for the post laundry. Wednesdays he loaded the folded sheets on a two-and-a-half-ton truck, rode to the laundry and unloaded them. Thursdays he rode the empty truck to the laundry, loaded up clean sheets, rode back to his company supply room, and passed out clean sheets. For the Saturday half-day's duty, he was supernumerary. That meant he tried to look busy around the supply room; if he failed, they sent him over to the dayroom to help the orderly clean up to get ready for the weekend. Off-duty at noon each Saturday—unless he came up on the rosters for KP or guard mount—he spent his weekends wandering on the post.

He sat in the Service Club, because it was air-conditioned, and because he could hide behind a magazine and watch the Special Service girls—blondes, redheads, tall women who wore high heels and stockings with seams up the backs of their long legs; he could smell their perfume when they passed close to him. He pretended to read, watched them conducting bingo games and Ping-Pong tournaments. He drank coffee and Cokes in the big snack bar over at Camp Funston. He tried reading books in the post library, but his English was not good enough to read much. He drank 3.2 beer at the outdoor tables at the central PX, but he got sick easily on too much cold beer, and his head ached in the hot Kansas sun with all that beer inside him. Sometimes he walked all the way over to Camp Forsythe to watch the guard mount at the post stockade, found a spot of shade and watched the prisoners file in and out on fatigue details, armbands with a big black letter P, the guards with their shotguns and lacquered helmet liners that reflected the bright sunlight.

He wished he was a stockade guard so he could carry a shotgun, get one of those special helmet liners. He had heard guards got an automatic transfer if they shot an escaping prisoner. If he was a stockade guard, Henry Peña thought, he would get a transfer, get to be someplace else, be something else instead of the one who had to shake out the dirty sheets for all of division headquarters at Fort Riley, Kansas. Sometimes he even wished he was a prisoner, wore an armband, marched in and out of Forsythe's old limestone cavalry barns that were the stockade barracks now.

He tried lying. Monday mornings, when the other men in Quartermaster Company complained about their hangovers and talked about the women they had in Manhattan and Junction City and Lawrence and Topeka and Kansas City, he tried with them. He said, "You guys got to go all the way off to Kansas City to get you some. Me, I got me womens right in Junction City and Manhattan, see? I go in and stay all weekend, this one I got even pays for my beer I drink."

"Sure thing, Pena," one man said to him.

"You hear this?" another said. "Pena gets all he wants right here close to home. Must be you tapping all them sorority girls at K-state, right, Pena?"

"If he is he wasn't this weekend," said another, "since I happen to have personally saw him walking around like a lost dog over at Funston when I was coming back from Junction City in a cab. You got a woman lives on the post, Pena?"

"Pena," another said to him, "you could make a fortune selling that crap for fertilizer, man."

"Hey, Pena," a man said, "tell the truth for once in your life. You ever really ever slept with a woman in your whole damn life?"

So there was not even anyone he could lie to.

Evenings, he sat alone at the EM Club, sipped a glass of 3.2 beer, listened in on all the drunken stories told by men who had been in Korea, stories about fighting the Chinese and the gook Koreans, stories about whores, Japanese women. Listening, he finally got his idea about how to make a lie that would work.

He was listening to two men talking one night, late in July. One was an older man; he looked as old as the man who lived with Henry Peña's mother but was not his real father. The older man was a corporal. The other man was much younger, only a few years older than Henry; on his sleeve were the fresh impressions of corporal's stripes only recently removed; the younger man had been busted down for something. They were both so drunk they could barely keep their heads off the table while they argued.

They argued about the use of the 60 mm. mortar. The younger man said, "I been on crew-serve weapons all my life, and now you're going to tell me from mortars?" The older man smiled, reached into his pocket and pulled out a Combat Infantryman's Badge, held it up to show to the younger man; it had the star between the tips of the wreath, which Henry Peña knew meant the man had been in two wars. The younger man snorted, said, "Seventy-five cents in the damn PX." Both men laughed. They talked about a whorehouse in a place near Pusan they had both visited, and Henry Peña had his idea about how to make a lie work.

Henry Peña figured he needed two things to make a lie work: proofs, something that would look like proofs, and the right person to tell the lie to. After that, it was the telling it, telling the lie right so it would be believed, as real as anything real.

Getting proofs was the easiest part. He had to wait two weeks to do it, because he drew KP the next weekend, and then he had to wait to the end of the month for payday. Then, with his money in his pocket, he took the shuttle bus into Junction City. He was careful. He waited until it was dark, all the troops from Fort Riley off the streets, socked in for the night at the 3.2 bars and the private bottle clubs and the VFW hall.

It was only a few minutes before closing time that he entered the biggest of the three military supply and surplus stores to buy what he needed. He worried the clerk might ask him what he wanted the stuff for, but it was easy. He picked it out, paid his money, and took it back to Fort Riley on the shuttle, stashed it in his wall locker behind his issue fatigue uniforms.

Henry Peña bought a set of gabardines, because issue khakis never held creases any longer than it took to start sweating in the Kansas heat; all the good soldiers, sharp soldiers, owned a set of gabardines for summer wear. He bought a pair of custom jumpboots because issue boots never took a good spit shine; he could spit shine the toes and heels of his new boots until they looked like they were dipped in glass. And custom jump boots had the double sole and heel paratroopers wore.

He bought the airborne patch for his garrison cap, the blue infantryman's cord, infantry collar brass, and a custom belt buckle, coated so it was not necessary to use Brasso to get a high gloss on it. Then he picked out the badges and the ribbons.

He got a Presidential Unit Citation for his right breast pocket, a Combat Infantryman's Badge, a parachutist's badge, and two rows of ribbons to go under them on his left breast: National Defense, Korean Service Ribbon with the two battle stars, Purple Heart, Bronze Star with V for valor, Good Conduct, Japanese Occupation, and the Syngman Rhee Citation. He bought two hashmarks for his left sleeve, two gold combat-time bars for his right, the ones they called chocolate bars, and staff sergeant chevrons. For his right shoulder, he bought the patch of the 5th Regimental Combat Team, because he had seen a man with that who also wore the parachutist's badge.

Now he had the proofs he needed to make his lie work. He did his sewing late at night in the latrine, worrying someone would stumble in and catch him at it. But nobody did; a little luck was needed for a good lie to work.

He went to Manhattan, the Kansas State University campus, to find the right person to tell it to. He carried his new uniform in a dry cleaner's bag, rode a taxi in to Aggieville, the strip of 3.2 bars on the edge of the K-State campus. In a Phillips 66 gas station restroom, he changed into his new liar's uniform, carried his civies out with him in a grocery sack rolled and tucked under his arm. And then Henry Peña, looking like a staff sergeant who had served with the 5th RCT in Korea, been wounded, decorated, a qualified paratrooper, walked in his new spit shined custom jump boots to the nearest beer bar, where the KSU students gathered, to find somebody, the right person, to tell his lie to.

It took awhile. He sat in The Huddle for nearly an hour, on a stool at the bar, looking at himself in his new uniform, his stripes, badges, ribbons, infantryman's cord, drinking draft 3.2. But there weren't any women in The Huddle. There were only college boys, dressed in cutoff sweatshirts and tee-shirts, shorts and tennis shoes without socks; they all sat at tables, drank pitchers of 3.2, laughing a lot. He overheard a couple of jokes told, but there was no one he could have talked to, so he sat alone at the bar, looked at himself in the mirror. When he ordered another draft, the bartender served him, took his money, made change without speaking. He put half a dollar in the jukebox, but did not recognize any of the songs he punched, and nobody at the tables seemed to hear the music he played.

When he ordered another draft, held his empty glass out to bring the bartender down from the other end of the bar, Henry Peña said to him, "Man, where is all the peoples?"

"End of summer school, Sarge," the bartender said as he drew on the tap.

Henry Peña did not understand what that meant, so he said, "Man, I mean how's come you don't got not even one womens in this place at night?"

"Oh," said the bartender, "if it's the bitches you're looking for, broads go mostly to Moxie's or Kampus Korner. You just move in out at Riley, Sarge?" he said. "Troops mostly go to J.C. for broads I'm saying. Your war suit there's as likely to scare off all the sorority gals, Sarge."

"Man," Henry Peña said, "don't tell me from how to get womens, see? I don't fight in the war in Korea and get shot up without I knew getting womens. You ever been to Japan, man, them womens in Japan?" he asked the bartender. The bartender shook his head no, but he leaned on his forearms on the bar, bent his head toward Henry Peña, ready to listen.

And Henry Peña almost began to tell about the women he had had in Japan, the fighting he had done in Korea, almost started to tell his lie, but he knew the bartender was not the right person, there in The Huddle with all the college boys drinking pitchers of 3.2, telling dumb jokes, dumb music playing on the jukebox, autographed photographs of KSU football players on the walls, pennants of all the schools in the Big Seven football conference. The place was not right, the bartender was not the right person—nothing would come of telling his lie here, nothing real happen. "Terrific stuff, man, the excellent gash in Japan," is all Henry Peña said to the bartender, and he paid for his last beer and left The Huddle.

He found Moxie's, and there were two women there, and even the bartender was an old woman; she reminded him of his mother back in Santa Fe. But the two women, college girls, were with their college boy boyfriends, two couples at two tables way back in the dark corners of Moxie's 3.2 bar. One couple sat side by side at a small table, fooling around, tickling each other, hugging, kissing little kisses. The other couple had their heads together over a table, whispering, kissing little kisses when they stopped whispering.

The old woman tending bar said to him, "Hi there, Sergeant. What brings you out here from the fort with the frat rats?" Henry Peña drank one draft 3.2, then left.

Now he was afraid he would not get to tell his new, big lie, that it was going to turn out just like the one about his rich father who owned a *rancho* in Old Mexico, the one about his *Pachuko* tattoos. He found a package store, went in and bought a fifth of Paul Jones. "Nearest private club's way to other side of the campus, Sarge," the clerk, an old man wearing a hearing aid and an aloha shirt, said.

"I drink it on the damn street," Henry Peña told him; at least the new uniform kept the clerk from asking him for proof of his age—at least that much worked.

He took the Paul Jones in a paper sack, took it out onto the deserted streets of Aggieville, cracked the seal, drank as much as his throat and stomach would take of the burn, sat on the curb, looked at the vacant street, what he could see of the unlit buildings on the KSU campus, the open greensward, occasional darker shapes of trees, lines of shrubbery.

Henry Peña sat with his fifth of Paul Jones, wondered what was going to happen to him in his life. The whiskey made him sad. He could hear some jukebox music coming from one of the bars on the Aggieville strip, and he heard the cicadas grinding in the grass and trees, a sound he had never heard in

Santa Fe. It sounded like the world laughing at him because all he was was a liar who could not tell any that worked. He felt the sticky weight of the humid air on his skin, the warm concrete under the seat of his gabardine trousers; the heat in Santa Fe was always dry, and the nights cooled there.

Henry Peña was very sad. He was in Kansas, and he was a bad liar, and if he could not even tell a good, big lie that worked, then he was never going to be anything, because a liar was all he had ever been, could be. The uniform cost him a lot of money, and all he had to show for it was a bottle of whiskey, and if he drank a lot of that he would get sick as hell. He threw the bag holding his civies into the gutter.

Then, for no reason, he got up from the curb and walked down the Aggieville strip, and at the corner he found himself standing in front of the Kampus Korner. And he went in, and there were women, college girls, lots of them, a lot of them with their college boys, but not all of them were—some sat at the bar, at tables, in twos and threes, even a few alone. And there, alone at a very small table, in the farthest corner from the door and the bar, drinking 3.2 beer by herself, as if she were the only person in the bar, Henry Peña found the right person to tell his lie to.

And the uniform worked. Some people stared at him when he went to the bar, and they moved aside to give him room, and he had two glasses of beer at the bar, and watched himself and everyone in the backbar mirror. And he saw how the woman, the college girl who sat all alone in the far corner, kept watching him. She kept watching him, the way a person watches someone or something he wants to touch, but does not dare. So when he got his third draft 3.2, Henry Peña went over to the college girl who sat alone at the very small table in the farthest corner of the Kampus Korner.

"Hey," Henry Peña said to her, "you looking all alone by yourself here. How abouts I sit down and we can talk or something, huh? I even got something special to drink here, we could share if you want," he said, and held up the fifth of Paul Jones in the paper sack. She looked up at him like she had not heard, or if she had, did not understand what he said. When she said nothing, he said, "Hey, you mind if I sit down here with you? It's crowded at the bar and my legs get tired if I stand too long." When she only looked at him, a surprised look on her face, as if the last thing she expected was someone speaking to her, wanting to sit with her, Henry Peña said, "See, I got shot in the legs with mortars and frostbite too, in Korea, so my legs hurt standing up so much, see?"

She said, "I guess you can if you want," and he took a free chair from the next table and sat down as close to her at the table as he could manage.

He expected her to say something then, but she looked away, down at the glass of flat beer she held with both hands. He almost got up and left, gave up on it, but the lie about his legs, wounds and frostbite from Korea, had gotten him the chair at her table, close to her, and so Henry Peña made up his mind to make it work.

"I'm Sergeant Henry Peña," he said, "You could tell me your name too so we could talk instead of just sit here, huh?"

"Cynthia," she said without looking up from her beer.

"Cynthia?" he said. "Hey, Cindy, right, that's a nice name. Cindy what?" He had to ask her to repeat her last name for him, because it was the kind of name he had never heard, nobody in Santa Fe or the army with a name like that.

"Von Eschen," she said, "Cynthia von Eschen."

"Cindy von Eschen. I'm Sergeant Henry Peña. Cindy von Eschen is a real nice name though. I like the name Cindy a lot."

"Nobody calls me Cindy," she said. "My folks always call me Cynthia, everybody at home, friends," she said.

"But I like Cindy better than Cynthia. Cindy sounds

nicer. I know somebody once name Cindy in Santa Fe. Santa Fe's my hometown before I join up the army, see? Where you coming from, Cindy?"

He let her talk a while before he started into his lie. She told him her hometown, and that she was a KSU freshman, that she was not in a sorority, but she did not care that she was not rushed, sororities were all cliques, and she hated cliques. Henry Peña did not know what a clique was. But he asked her enough questions to keep her talking; she told him she was homesick for her family and her hometown, wished she had not come to Manhattan to go to college at KSU, that she would be going home next week for a visit before she came back for the fall semester, only she might transfer to the University of Wisconsin, except that was also a big frat and sorority school, full of cliques too. He kept her talking, and he got her to drink up her beer, let him buy her another. He asked her if she wanted a drink of his Paul Jones whiskey, and she said she had only tasted whiskey once in her life and did not like the taste of it.

"Hey, you got to try it, Cindy. It don't taste so bad, but then you get all warm and nice all over, you feel good as hell, you don't care about nothing the way nothing is except you feel great, see? You don't even feel homesick no more, you get some whiskey down you. Me, I get homesick ever for Santa Fe, I drink some whiskies and don't worry about it none no more." He got her to tip up the fifth of Paul Jones, the neck sticking out of the paper sack. She choked on it, but got it down, and he promised her it would feel great if she would just wait a minute. "I learn to drink whiskies when I was in the war fighting in Korea," he told her.

"Is that what all that means?" she said, pointing at the ribbons on his chest. "I know your stripes means you're a sergeant, but what's all that for?" Then Henry Peña really began to tell her his lie.

She listened, and she asked questions at the right times,

and he got her to drink up her beer, bought her another. He got her to admit the drink of whiskey had begun to make her feel good, and then he got her to take another small drink.

"See," he told her, "I never got to school or college away from home and all, like you, because I joined up the army to fight in the war in Korea. I was real young, join up soon as I'm seventeen, and I been in the army ever since, which is why I'm a sergeant, see, and how I got wounded and got all these medals here I'm wearing now."

"School's not so great," she said. "College stinks. KSU stinks. Wisconsin probably stinks just as much. Everyone's a snob or part of a clique. College is even more boring than high school."

She was not a good-looking woman. Henry Peña thought he liked women who were tall and had big chests; he liked long legs on a woman, big thighs, and he liked long blonde hair on a woman, or redheads, big dark eyes, big red lips. This Cindy funny-last name was pretty tall, but she was thin; she had real thin arms and legs, and almost no chest he could see looking down her blouse, and her hair was short and brown except she tied it in a little tail in the back; she had little eyes, and hardly any lips at all. He wondered if he would like kissing her. "How's come you squint, is it your eyes hurt?" he asked her.

"I got new contacts," she said.

But she smelled nice, like clean sheets when he put his head very close to hers to talk to her; she smelled clean, and she had clean white fingernails, and her clothes were clean, smelled clean. She was the right person to tell his lie to, and he was sure he could make something happen from it.

"See," Henry Peña said to her, "I was in Korea with the 5th RCT. I was there for all the fighting. I got wounded in the legs, like I say before, and then I was a prisoner from the Chinese for over a year, too. This one here," he said, touching his Purple Heart ribbon, "is for when I get wounded."

"Really?" Cindy von Eschen said. "I was in high school

when I used to read about Korea, or even junior high maybe. It's funny sitting here in Aggieville talking to someone who was there when I was in junior high. How did you get hurt?" she asked him.

"Drink your beer up, I get you another one. This 3.2 ain't no real beer like you get in Santa Fe or in Korea and Japan I had. Drink it all up, we have us a little taste more of my whiskey, don't you feel real good already from it?" Henry Peña said.

They finished their beers, and he bought two more at the bar, and they each tipped the fifth of Paul Jones up again. She admitted to him she could feel it; she said it made her hands and feet warm and light. "I'll probably get drunk for the first time," she said, and laughed. "I've never been drunk ever before in my life," she said.

"You learn to like it like I did when I'm in Japan and fighting the war in Korea. You get drunk, you don't think no more about all your trouble you got," he said. And then Henry Peña told her all about getting his wounds in Korea. It was the biggest lie he ever told.

It was the right place for it. The college boys and their college girls crowded the bar, at tables, talking loud, laughing, giving each other little hugs and little kisses, played their dumb music on the jukebox. What he said, only she heard. She put her head close to his to be able to hear; he smelled the good smell of her very white skin, her clean brown hair. She was not fine looking; she was almost ugly, but she was the right person to tell a lie to. She wanted to hear it, and she wanted to believe it, and as he told it it sounded more real than any other lie he had ever told, as real as who he really was, anything he had ever really done. When he glanced up at the Kampus Korner crowd, he felt himself a real staff sergeant with airborne badges and ribbons and combat decorations. When he looked into Cindy von Eschen's small squinting eyes he saw that he was a real staff sergeant, telling her about his war in Korea, as real to himself as he was to her.

What he said was easy. Things he had heard listening to soldiers who had been there came into his head to say, like they were his own memories. When he stopped talking to drink his beer, something always came to him to say.

"When I got wounded," he said, "it was winter. Terrible cold and all snow on the ground. You could freeze to death even if the Chinese guys don't shoot you," he said.

"We have the worst winters in the world in Wisconsin," she said.

"Sure, but this is terrible winter in Korea, fighting. Some people freeze to death, or their feet they have to cut off. We live in big trenches and tents and little holes we dig in the trenches. We got all barb wire to keep Chinese away, see? When they come at us at night, you hear them jiggle the wire. We shoot up flares and you can see them all coming through the wire. Then we shoot the hell out of them."

"How does it feel? When you shoot somebody."

"I like it," Henry Peña said. "See, it's like real exciting. You forget it all except to shoot the hell out of them because they trying to kill you too. Drink up your beer, Cindy."

"I'm afraid I'll get sick," she said.

"Never happen," he said, and he got her to taste the whiskey again. And he told her about the bugles the Chinese blew when they attacked, and about how he sighted his Browning Automatic Rifle on the Chinese in their padded coats, caught in the wire. "You know what they wear for shoes, Cindy? Regular sneaks, man. Honest, sneaks they wear for shoes in winter!" He told her about the mortars, how incoming sounded different that outgoing, about the one that hit close and cut up his legs with fragments.

"It must feel different to be you," she said. "I mean it must be something you could have had dreams about if you think about it a lot."

"I don't let nothing bother me," Henry Peña said, and told her then about how the Chinese overran his trench; he could not get up and run because he was hit in the legs, so they caught him there. "They shoot everybody what can't walk, so I make myself get up and walk off with them. I was bleeding like hell in the snow, real cold, see?" He told her about being a prisoner of war, how he nearly froze and starved to death before he was repatriated, all the bonus money he got, his rest and recuperation leave in Japan. And he kept her drinking her beers, got her to taste the whiskey again. He was going to tell her about the women in Japan, make it real for her, for himself.

"I have to go potty," she said, and got up, went to the ladies' rest room that said *Dolls* on the door. He waited for her, had some more whiskey, sat there in the Kampus Korner, Aggieville, Kansas, and he felt it was all very real—himself, Korea, his badges and stripes and ribbons, more real than the noisy college boys and their college girls, Fort Riley, the supply room where he worked shaking out and folding dirty sheets, Santa Fe, as real as Luis Roybal, who was a real paratrooper in Kentucky someplace.

When she came back to the table, he could see the drinking had gotten to her. Her face was even more pale, a light sweat on her forehead and cheeks and throat.

"Have you some more whiskey," he said. "It makes you feel better if it's bothering you and you just stay drinking it, you get better real soon."

"I better go," she said; when she stood up, she almost fell on the table.

"I can take you someplace," Henry Peña said, and walked her to the bar; her arm felt clammy as he helped her. He held her up while the bartender called a taxi for them.

The Kampus Korner bartender said, "Looks like you got you a problem with that little girlie, Sarge."

"Man," Henry Peña told him, "I know how to handle the womens, see?" Cindy von Eschen was able to walk out to the taxi when it came, but when Henry Peña tried talking to her, she only mumbled. The instant he got her in the taxi, she passed out. "Man," he said to the driver, "what's a room close to here?"

The taxi driver flipped on the dome light, twisted to lean back over the seat, looked at Henry Peña, Cindy von Eschen passed out, head lolling. "That's jailbait there, Sarge, looks like to me." The driver made a clucking sound with his tongue.

"Hey," Henry Peña said, "are you telling me about the womens, man? Don't tell me nothing about womens. I been at womens all over the world in Korea and Japan, see?" The driver shrugged, turned back to the wheel, hit the meter flag. "Just find me some room I can get for us, huh?"

They drove, and Henry Peña felt the driver's eyes watching him in the rearview mirror; Henry Peña held her up when Cindy von Eschen started to fall over, worried about the taxi meter clicking away as they drove the dark, empty streets of Manhattan, if he would have enough money for the fare, a room, a taxi back to Fort Riley. He held Cindy von Eschen up on the backseat; something real was happening out of his lie. He felt like telling the driver about the women of Korea and Japan, what he had heard from other soldiers about whores who worked in filthy cribs in places like Seoul and Pusan, scented Japanese whores who gave baths and massages and worked in rooms with round beds, tinted mirrors set in the ceilings, Tokyo, Eta Jima. What he had heard from other men came to him like sharp memories.

The motel the driver took them to was called the Blue Court, a big blue neon sign, small cabins ranged along a gravel drive, a blue lightbulb over each cabin door. "Wait while I get a room, huh?" he said to the driver.

"It's your party, Sarge," the driver said without turning to him.

The desk clerk was just a young kid, half-asleep at a card table, a television on with the sound turned off. "All night?" he asked Henry Peña as he got the key, peered out the window at the waiting taxi.

"What's the differences, man?"

"Twenty if you stay to check-out, otherwise fifteen if it's just a hot bed you need." The kid grinned at him. Henry Peña checked his wallet; he had more than forty dollars left. "Sweet dreams," the kid said, laughed, when Henry Peña gave him a twenty.

"Man," he said to the kid, "I ain't doing no dreaming. I'm for turning the bitch every which way except loose." He laughed with the kid.

When he paid off the taxi, pulled and lifted Cindy von Eschen out, stood her on her feet, teetering and mumbling about feeling sick, the driver said, "Ain't hardly no challenge if they're half-dead drunk, is it, Sarge."

"Man," he said, holding her up, cabin key in his hand, "I sober the bitch up first, see? I done this times before."

He half-dragged, half-carried her to the cabin, propped her against the door while he fumbled the key into the lock under the blue light. Her face and bare arms, her legs, were blue in the light, and he suddenly felt all the whiskey and 3.2 beer flip in his stomach, rush in his head. He looked at his blue hands working the key in the lock.

Cindy von Eschen almost fell into the room when the door opened. Just as he caught her by the waist, she vomited all over the doorsill.

"Goddamn, woman, you got to do that in the toilet," he said; the smell rose up to his nose, filled the small room even after he got her inside, door closed. He let her fall on the bed while he turned on the light. He felt sick, now, could not keep from staggering as he lurched to the tiny bathroom to throw up. He flushed the toilet, looked at himself in the mirror, his sweated face, loud breath heaving his chest and shoulders, his wrinkled uniform. "Okay," he said to himself in the bathroom mirror, "now you ready for it, Sergeant Henry Peña."

He stripped off his uniform, the badges and brass, chevrons, medals, hashmarks, threw them in a heap on the dirty floor. "Come on, baby, you," he said to Cindy von Eschen, but she lay face down on the bed, snoring, did not speak. "Hey," he said, rolled her over, "now for it," but her eyes were closed, arms limp. The smell of her vomit hit him again, and his vision blurred. "Bitch Cindy," he said, "I get you straight like six o'clock here!"

He took off her clothes, struggling with her flopping arms and legs, the bed shifting under them, barely able to make his fingers unbutton her buttons, unzip her zipper. "Damn," he said, his head whirling, "you skinny like a little boy, you ain't got no chest. Stink," he said, because the smell of her vomit was still on her, even with all her clothes off.

"I get you straight," he said as he pulled her off the bed, across the floor to the bathroom, her bare heels dragging. He did his best to get her into the bathtub without knocking her head against it. He stood over her a moment before he turned on the water; she looked like a little boy, asleep, curled up in the bottom of the bathtub.

He turned on the water, then had to find the knob that changed it to a shower. He stood up to watch the shower running hard, and did not know anything was wrong until he saw the steam all around him, filling the tiny bathroom. Then she began to scream.

He could hear her bare arms and legs smacking against the tub, screaming louder and louder. He stood there in the swirling steam, felt the searing heat of the water, hearing her screaming before he could think to try to find the faucet, turn it off. He groped in the cloud of scalding steam, yelled when the water hit his hands and arms.

Henry Peña could not find the faucet. He could only stand there, naked, hear her scream, and then he heard the pounding on the cabin door, and he tried to think what to do, what he could say, but nothing came to him, and he was still standing there when she stopped screaming, someone broke in the cabin door, grabbed him, threw him out of the tiny bathroom. He ended up on the dirty floor by the bed, wet, sick, unable to open his eyes; he felt around with his hands for the heap of his clothes, the uniform, but could not find them, and he could not think of any lie to tell that anyone would believe.

———◆———

What does my story mean?

It means: all fictions are lies, however much truth goes into the making of them; a fiction writer is a liar, who, to make his fictions work, has to use his imagination and his skill with language to transform elements of the truth into a lie a reader can believe; if a fiction works, the lie is well told, then it becomes real, the truth again, because the reader is not who he was anymore when he believes something new.

It means everything is language, that anything that is real—the truth—is real only in the substance of the language that embodies it. And so the reason there will always be fictions is because fiction writers, like me, want very much to make real things, and to make real things last.

A successful fiction endures, but does not satisfy the fiction writer's need; there will always be something, someone, some words spoken, or not spoken, that must be made real, turned into a lie that somebody—if only the fiction writer himself—can believe.